A Deadly Pipeline

A Deadly Pipeline

J. K. NEAL

LifeRich Publishing is a registered trademark of The Reader's Digest Association, Inc.

LifeRich Publishing books may be ordered through booksellers or by contacting:

LifeRich Publishing
1663 Liberty Drive
Bloomington, IN 47403
www.liferichpublishing.com
1 (888) 238-8637

Because of the dynamic nature of the Internet, any web addresses or links contained in this book may have changed since publication and may no longer be valid. The views expressed in this work are solely those of the author and do not necessarily reflect the views of the publisher, and the publisher hereby disclaims any responsibility for them.

Any people depicted in stock imagery provided by Thinkstock are models, and such images are being used for illustrative purposes only.
Certain stock imagery © Thinkstock.

Scripture taken from the King James Version of the Bible.

This is a work of fiction. All of the characters, names, incidents, organizations, and dialogue in this novel are either the products of the author's imagination or are used fictitiously.

ISBN: 978-1-4897-1464-0 (sc)
ISBN: 978-1-4897-1463-3 (hc)
ISBN: 978-1-4897-1462-6 (e)

Library of Congress Control Number: 2017917893

Print information available on the last page.

LifeRich Publishing rev. date: 11/20/2017

A DEADLY PIPELINE

By J. K. Neal

A short story of colorful characters, ancient history, intrigue, and a treasure.

CL Wilkerson was a successful business man having attained every goal he ever set out to achieve. So, his days became a quest for the next big score. But little did he know how this adventure would affect his life and everything in it.

CONTENTS

A DISCRIPTION OF TERMS AND THE PIPELINER'S VERNACULAR

The pipeline industry has its own unique terms and sayings. So, if you have never been exposed to pipeliner's lingo before here is an abbreviated list of terms that appear in this story for reference

RIGHT OF WAY	The easement purchased by the pipeline owner and also, the limit of disturbance to build the pipeline
HAND	This term has two meanings: The first is in reference to any worker on a pipeline The second is in reference to an exceptional worker as in "he is a real hand"
SPREAD	The complete set of men and equipment required to build a pipeline
BOOM	A crawler tractor with an A frame attached to the left side used to pick up pipe. Its correct name is a "Side Boom"
HOE	A reference to a Tracked Backhoe

STRINGING	The act of pre-positioning the pipe on the right of way Unloaded from semi-trucks and placed near the ground and on "skids" so that it can be assembled and welded
SKIDS	4"x 6" by 42" long rectangular lumber used to temporarily support the pipe
JOINTS	Lengths of pipe that typically are 40 feet long but also, can come in 20, 60 and 80-foot lengths
LOADING TERMINAL	The end of the onshore pipeline and where ships are loaded with oil
DITCH	The excavated trench that the pipeline is eventually placed in
LOWER IN	Placing the welded, inspected, and coated pipeline sections in the trench completed with side booms
COATING	Anti-corrosive coating applied to the pipeline after welding but prior to placing it in the ditch
TIE INS	Once the pipeline sections are in the trench they are welded together or tied in
BACKFILL	This term has a dual meaning: The first is the spoil pile generated from the trench excavation The second is covering up the trench after the pipe is placed in it

WELDER HUTS	The tents used in a mechanized welding process positioned with a smaller side boom and placed over the pipeline prior to welding to keep wind and adverse conditions from affecting the weld and welding process
DRAG UP	Quit the project
RUNOFF	Be fired from the project
PIGs	Cylindrical devices just smaller than the internal dimeter of the pipeline used to both check the internal integrity of the pipeline and to clean the pipeline prior to the introduction of Oil and are loaded and receive in temporarily installed devices

THE CROWN

GOLDEN CUFF

GOLDEN CRUCIFIX

THE INNER BOX

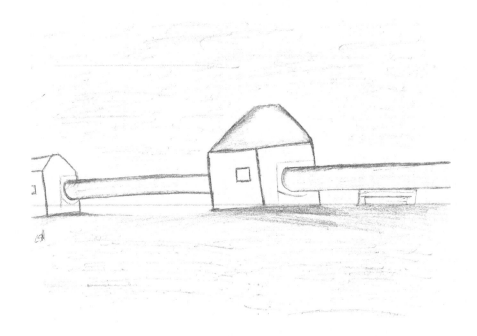

WELDER SHACKS

A PIPELINE "PIG"

THE LOST TREASURE
OF DAMASCUS

In 634 AD "Damascus was the first major city of the Byzantine Empire, the old Roman empire to fall in the Muslims during their conquest of Syria. Mohammad who started Islam died in 632 so Abu Bakr became his successor in 634. Abu Bakr invaded and laid siege to Damascus in 634 AD. The city was taken after a Christian bishop in hopes of gaining favor with the enemy informed one of the Muslim generals, that it was possible to breach the city walls by attacking a position at the Eastern gate that was only lightly defended at night.

While the Muslim army entered the city by assault from the Eastern gate, the commander of the Byzantine garrison, negotiated a peaceful surrender at a different gate with Abu Bakr. The city surrendered peacefully. After the surrender, the commanders from each side disputed the terms of the peace agreement. The commanders finally agreed that the peace terms would be met if the Byzantines would depart from the city and leave all their goods and possessions behind.

The peace terms included an assurance that the Muslims would not pursue the departing Byzantine convoy for at least three days. As the Muslims entered the city and as the Byzantines were departing it became evident to the Muslim invaders that all things of any value had been stripped bare and taken with them. But in fact all of the valuables were placed in a gopher wood box and smuggled out of the city the night before the main body of the refugees departed. The Muslim invaders had no idea of the extent of valuables in the treasure box that had left the city. But bound to the peace terms, it was three days after the surrender of the city that the Muslim army set out after these" Damascene Roman " refugees and their belongings. The Muslim army caught up with them and defeated them in a battle six days later, near present day Al Jayyad in Northern Syria. But no valuables were ever recovered.

As it turns out that a separate party carrying the valuables went a different direction to that of the main group of refugees. The main body of refugees went North and travelled about 175 miles toward Al Jayyad but the valuables went West of the city and were buried in a very obscure location. They buried the box hastily and marked with a few stones and left it in the desert. The trouble was about marking things in the desert that way is that the ever-shifting sand and sand dunes could obscure the markers. Things are easily lost to the desert. **And so, it was.**

It is assumed that the party after hiding the treasure returned with the main body of fleeing refugees somewhere before they reached Al Jayyad. And if they did they were killed with all the others either in the battle of Al Jayyad or during the ensuing mass executions that followed. So, It is not certain whether any Byzantines survived and ever returned to recover the hoard. But even If anyone ever returned they were unable to find the location of their buried treasure.

Some nomads who were camping nearby witnessed the burial of something but they could not determine what it was. So, the existence of a treasure became very speculative from the beginning. A sand storm started late that same afternoon. By the next day when the nomads were sure the party was gone and not just waiting for them to start digging before they were ambushed tried to find the location. They tried for 3 days to find the exact spot but by this time it had already been lost to the dessert. So, it was never found. Since it was assumed that all of the Byzantines had been killed in battle or executed thereafter, then that left only the Muslims who knew things had disappeared from Damascus. And even they had no idea of the extent of the valuables. For if they had they would have probably put forth more effort in trying to locate it. The Muslims encountered the nomads on the way back to Damascus and learned about the burial. But they dug a few holes and became disinterested very quickly. Besides there were other cities in Syria waiting to be conquered and killing a few Romans and taking their belongings seemed to be much easier than digging holes anyway.

So, the treasure lay there undiscovered for over 1300 years.

CHAPTER ONE

The Deal of a Lifetime

RYIADH Saudi Arabia

The OPEC council was meeting at the Amir's palace. With all the member nations representatives in attendance. All of them were clothed in the traditional Middle Eastern garb. The order of the day was to try and figure out how to increase oil production revenues due to the recently ridiculously low oil prices. It had been rumored that Iran was about to flood the market even further and gain further market share on the others. This however was not discussed at the meeting since Iran was an OPEC member, it had its representatives at the meeting, and it was not really the venue for this type of confrontation to take place.

The ticker on the wall that displayed the current oil prices seemed to be spinning lower each second so that it resembled more like an airplane altimeter in a nose dive than it did a ticker. The participants were at odds on just exactly what to do, and in typical Arab fashion, the meeting resembled a riot more than a meeting with each sheik trying to out talk and over talk the other. Finally, Sheik Nasser Al-Issa of Saudi Arabia jumped to his feet angrily grabbed the gavel from across the table out of the hand of another and started pounding it on the table trying to get the attention of all the others. "Brothers" "Bothers he shouted we need order!". Eventually the room fell silent.

Then he started to speak in a very quiet and soft tone to the group. "We must increase our capacity" he began as he stepped away from the table and began walking behind the seated. We must" it's the only way." "We cannot do this" the foreign minister from Bahrain stood up and interjected. "All the pipelines are at capacity and are full..."No" "No" as he restated his position "they are over capacity " We cannot introduce more oil because we run the risk of a pipeline failure if we increase the pressure anymore" "We are already falsifying the pressure logs to get around our own government regulations"

"I'm not talking about an increase in that way, said Nasser "we must build additional capacity, we must build a large pipeline and we must do it quickly" "That would take two years to plan and build" said one of the group. "Well maybe not" said Nasser "I know a guy in Houston who just might be able to pull this off and put us in production by the end of the year. We will of course will need to go around our own regulations, but it is in our collective best interest"

"Do you have a design? Someone asked, "We can and will provide a design on the fly" said Nasser. "I know a guy" he said "So please confirm to us Nassar that we are trusting you and your" guys" to get this done by the years end is that it?" "yes, you are" said Nassar. "And materials"? Another responded

"I have a plan" said Nassar "These "guys" that you refer to are they American? Because if they are I'm telling you they cannot be trusted" " They will tell you anything you want to hear" said another Amir. "Do we really have much choice?" Nasser asked, "I mean other than to trust them?" There was no response from the group. "Then its settled I'll contact them right away" The over intense aura hovering over the room gave way to an uneasy confidence. The meeting concluded with the usual Arab cheek kisses and man hugs.

HOUSTON TEXAS USA

The phone rang at the CL Wilkerson Pipeline Construction Company. The very attractive 25-year-old receptionists answered, "CL Wilkerson Pipeline may I help you?". "Yes, I would like to talk to CL please" spoke the voice on the other end of the line in a thick Arabic accent.

"I'm sorry he is out of the office may I take a message?" "This is Nassar Al-Issa of the Kingdom of Saudi Arabia and I need to talk to CL right away please" " Oh I'm sorry sir he is on vacation and is out of the country" she said rather apologetically.

"Then where is he staying madam?" "It is urgent" Nassar said in a short and impatient tone "He is in St Martin staying at the Belmond La Samanna hotel" Would you like his cell number to try it as well?" "Yes" was the reply "It is 712-444-1000 but I don't believe he has very good service down there". " I have been trying to get though all day myself" "Well thank you very much for your time and your help, good day" said Nasser as he hung up the phone. Immediately googling "Belmond La Samanna" to get the phone number.

ST MAARTEN

The steward came walking down from the hotel to the beachfront to inform him about the phone call. Laying in a lounge chair clad in a red speedo was the 56-year-old CL Wilkerson. Beside him was an absolutely gorgeous 25-year-old blonde who had been a model in her earlier twenties but seemed now to be content to just be in line to someday be the future 4th ex-wife of CL Wilkerson. "Mr. Wilkerson there is an urgent phone call for you in the hotel sir." The steward said as he stood in front of the chair his back to the sinking sun. "Who the hell even knows I'm here? That damn Sherrie has let the cat out of the bag again"

"Ok show me the way son" "I'll be right back Carolyn" CL said as he grabbed his man bag. They made their way through the sand of the beach toward the hotel. CL looked down at the sand and it reminded him of his most profitable project to date. 600 miles of 42"-inch pipeline in Saudi Arabia. He had made 200 million dollars on that deal. "Yeah I could damn sure use another one of those" he muttered to himself as they made their way off the beach and into the hotel.

The steward pointed to a private room with French doors off to the heft. "You can take your call in there sir" The room was small but had 12-foot ceilings and cherry wood paneled walls. There was an arm chair and a desk with a funky old European style telephone sitting on its top. "I'll get the switchboard to connect you" the steward said as he left the room. CL reached in his bag and pulled out one of his favorite cigars. An Partagas Black label bravo. As he lit the cigar the phone rang. CL sat on the desk as he picked up the phone. "CL Wilkerson here ...who is this?" "CL I'm glad I found you this is Nassar." "Nassar how in the hell are you?" CL exclaimed "I need you to come to Saudi right away because it is very important." Nassar said "OK sure Nassar but tell me what this is about" CL inquired "We need a long pipeline built and we need it in service before the end of the year" said Nassar. "Well let's see... Can you answer a few questions for me Nassar? " Like what size, how long, and where the hell at?" CL questioned.

"From Kuwait to Beirut." Nassar said sheepishly." "Oh brother, now Nasar don't try to bullshit a bull-shitter, there ain't no way you and you're A-rab friends could agree on that." CL always pronounced the word Arab with emphasis on the "A." " I mean you, Israel, Syria

4

and Lebanon all agree on anything? Sure. I'm not buying this plan Nassar." CL said.

"No, it's true. Iran is taking their extra oil production down to the Gulf We are not supposed to know this. And with the extra revenue they generate it will either fund terror groups or develop their nuclear program or both. So, as a countermeasure, and to not let Iran know what for sure we are up to we need to end our pipeline somewhere besides the Gulf or the Straight. We have agreements with Israel Syria, Jordan, and Lebanon already in place." His speech was a little faster and more intense than usual.

"This line starts in Kuwait and follows the Iraq border with us and then crosses through Jordan East of Amman and follows the Israeli border heading North crosses into Syria and then It continues to the West of Damascus crossing into Lebanon and ending at the port in Beirut. " Isn't Syria on the brink of Civil War Nassar? "I'm afraid so CL and that's why it's so urgent we get this line built right away" Nassar said "What about loading facilities in Beirut?" Quizzes CL. "don't worry I will take care of that" said Nassar. "Are you sure Nassar?" CL said " Now Nassar I'm not coming over there and busting my ass to get your pipeline built only to find out it can't be placed in service because you had some numb nutted A-rab contractor who can't keep his shit together" "Well I may have to have you intervein if the schedule starts to slip too badly" Nasar said. " I thought so". "But OK that's a good enough answer " said CL.

Now CL Wilkerson just bluffed his way into more work and money because there was not a snowballs chance in hell that he was going to walk away from this deal over its in-service date or for any other reason. He could really care less if it went in service on time, or at all for that matter. His greed was about to overtake him as it had done many times before.

"Well outside of the fact that that is the most hotly contested border in the World, and to follow that border with a pipeline route is not a good plan at all Nassar. I need to be up front with you on that. I mean Geeze Louise it would be crookeder than a dog's leg" "How do you expect to pull this off? Don't you think it may be just a little bit difficult to camouflage the construction of a big ass pipeline in the middle of the desert?" Do you even know which border with Israel are you talking about? The one on the East or the West?" CL said.

"We have a cover story in place for the construction of most of this pipeline or at least until it reaches Damascus." "No one in the Middle East wants to see Iran increase their output to use those funds for their rocket program". "So, you see CL this is an agreement out of necessity and I don't expect to have any country problems". "We will follow the East border with Israel". "I have already contacted Mr. Bob and he is looking for materials already." Said Nassar "Well that's a good start, Nassar." "Mr. Bob is a good as they come." Alright I'll pack up and be there by tomorrow afternoon, fair enough? Same arraignment as before?" Said CL. "Yes, same as before" said Nasser.

As CL hung up he called for the steward. "I need you to go down to the beach and tell Carolyn to get packed, we are leaving in an hour" "Yes sir" said the steward. Now if CL Wilkerson were capable of doing cartwheels He would have done so on the spot. He didn't do any cartwheels but he did however dance a little jig as he walked up to his room to pack. His mind was racing with the thoughts of another big score in Saudi. He had achieved great success in his career, But the success did not absolve all the passed issues he had with his father when it came to the company. If only his father was around to see this. That would really make it complete.

Things were never good between he and his father. His father was a great man, an innovator, a captain of the pipeline industry, and a philanthropist. And he viewed his son as an indecisive, spoiled child. Who had neither a trade nor a profession nor any real ambition. CL the third liked to party, chase women, and drive fast cars and all somewhere other than his native Texas. It wasn't until after his father's passing did he step up and take control of the company his grandfather had built in the early 1900's.

LONDON

The phone rang at 23 Burnham Road in Dartford near greater London. A man picked up the phone and heard a voice say, "Mr. Bob how in the hell, are you?" Mr. Bob replied in his thick welsh accent, "Why CL to what do I owe the pleasure?" CL curtly said, "You know very well why I'm calling you Bob you phony son of a bitch I just talked to Nassar". Mr. Bob Chuckled and said, "Now CL is that anyway to address a partner?" "Not a partner I think the word you are looking for is vendor" CL said again very curtly this time. "Well you may just want to visit with Nassar again CL because you can't lay it if I don't get it. The pipe that is". "So Nassar has made me a full partner on this one. Cheer up ol boy they are in a bind for this pipeline and they will pay us whatever we ask. So, your early completion bonus money will be safe and your money doggie bag will be full when you go home. I promise."

"Having any luck finding the pipe Bob?" CL asked. "Why CL I've already called all the major suppliers and have advised them of the premium Nassar is willing to pay and I don't think we will have any trouble getting materials, but worst case it will just be coming from many different sources and you will have many different lengths of pipe CL that's all." But it's going to push many people out of the queue and really piss some people off." Mr. Bob said. "Well I don't care about that. "just remember not to bring any of that cheap ass Chinese crap Bob do you hear?" "OK I understand CL." "Well, Cherrie-O Bob." "Call me in a week and let me know how you're doing" CL said. "Cheers" said Bob as they both hung up.

CHAPTER TWO

The Wilkerson Legacy

Cornelius Langhorne Wilkerson the first, the original Cornelius started in the pipeline business in 1924. He had worked for pipeline contractors since he was 14 starting in 1904 as a day laborer. Which meant you needed to show up each morning to find out if there was going to be any work for you that day.

This was back when the very first pipeline he worked on consisted of the installation of hollowed out tree trunks of 6 or 8 inches in diameter that were held together with steel banding material and laid in a hand dug trench to make gas lines. Gas mains had been laid this way since commercial gas was used in the late 1800's.

Cornelius, I was a smart ambitious young man with little formal education. By the time he was 34 he had started his own company and he never looked back. By the time his son Cornelius Langhorne Wilkerson II took over the company 30 years later in 1954 he was a multi-millionaire.

He had seen the industrial revolution come to the pipeline spreads. He had seen the advent of crawler tractors, the first use of diesel driven draglines. He saw the first use of steel pipe in

40-foot lengths or "joints" held together with mechanical "dresser couplings" and the use of acetylene welding on smaller pipe. Even the use of arc welding. He had seen the first use of an anti-corrosive coating applied to pipelines they called "hot dope" which came in 55-gallon drums that had to chopped with an axe and the pieces placed a heated pot to make it viscous called a "dope pot." By the time of his death he had built pipelines in 34 states and in Canada and Mexico.

Cornelius, I was a skinny, raw boned, whisky drinking, tobacco chewing, Pipe Liner who seemed to always be in overalls and wore a brown fedora. He was one of those who was always respectful to women, loved dogs and children and drank, chewed, and cussed every day of the week except Sunday.

He hated his given name Cornelius almost as much as his middle name. So, as you might guess that's why he went by his initials CL. And some say just to be mean he named his son Cornelius as well.

I guess that demeanor didn't get any better in the 2nd generation because it filtered down to his grandson Cornelius III. But one thing is for certain, name or no name, the first Cornelius certainly would not have approved of his grandson's exploits.

Cornelius II was well educated and took the company into the pipeline construction boom of the 1960's and 1970's. His father Cornelius I had raised him to have respect for others, and to appreciate his wealth. He had a focus in life at a very early age that he would one day take over the company his father had built and had loved. So, there was no doubt what his purpose in life was going to be. Cornelius, I died in 1954, and thereafter his son Cornelius II took on the company and enjoyed great success. He was shrewd with his clients and generous with his employees. He was humble even though his wealth surpassed 400 million dollars in a day when that was a tremendous amount of money. But his biggest failure in life was raising his only son Cornelius Langhorne Wilkerson III.

Cornelius III was a dandy, a lady's man, and a womanizer. He had turned out to be a girl chasing, pot smoking, whiskey drinking, Lamborghini driving, yacht sailing, tennis playing, ivy league smart-ass. He never met his grandfather but his father's stories about him seemed to keep him alive at least in Cornelius II heart if not Cornelius III. Cornelius III was such a smart ass after hearing the stories about his grandfather's reference to pipeline coating as" dope". He used to say, "Yeah pops don't tell me they didn't party and smoke weed on the pipeline back in grandpa's day because grandpa said dope came in 55-gallon drums and joints were 40 foot long!"

His father was certainly concerned about his son's ability to take over the company and with good reason. I guess that is why he worked every day until the day that he died. But he died just as he had lived. He died in 1994 on a pipeline right of way. He died on a chilly fall morning in New York on a pipeline spread drinking coffee before starting time and "shooting the shit with the hands as he loved to do". They said he had suffered a massive coronary and was dead before he hit the ground.

At the very same time Cornelius III was on a step ladder at his Houston home trying to retrieve a lawn chair from the roof of his house that found its way there during the previous night's drunk fest. As he reached for the chair he lost his balance and fell from the ladder to the concrete below breaking his hip. They said that the ambulances were called at the same time for both father and son.

Whether it was the fact that he could not attend his father's funeral or whether the accident made him realize his mortality is uncertain. But something made him change his ways and upon his recovery he stepped up and stepped in to his father's role.

CHAPTER THREE

CL Wilkerson III Takes Over

He made the most of his company's resources and built pipelines across the United States Canada and Mexico over the next several years. Some of the older hands finally concluded and stated that "the old man really did not have anything on the kid". Cornelius III had finally come into his own. And he became just as successful than his father had been.

He went against his father's intentions for the future of the company by taking on international projects. His father always said, "just because its far away from home doesn't mean it brings more money" But Cornelius III did have some moderate success in West Africa and South America. But his big score came when he did his first project in Saudi Arabia. He bribed his way to get an audience with the sheik Nassar Al-Issa. It seems that Cornelius's bullshit and rhetoric appealed to the sheik because he awarded him a $500 million-dollar project on the spot with out as much as an estimate.

The project went extremely well and it made CL some $200 million dollars. It went well thanks to the efforts of the best superintendent and assistant superintendent that the CL Wilkerson Pipeline

Construction Company had. Their names were AE Fontenot and Charles Simpson "three finger" Nixon.

AE was a slightly built Louisiana Cajun whose personality and demeanor endeared him to the hands and the clients alike. He was an up-beat down to earth plain-spoken man who had genuine charisma. He had been a rodeo clown in his earlier days and was short and wiry. It seems that some of the pipe liners don't care much for their given names and that's why they just go by their initials and he was no exception.

AE's mother was American by birth but raised as proper French. His father a rough and tumble Cajun whose family settled in Louisiana from France long before the Louisiana purchase. Her family had immigrated to America during world war 2 and had settled in Louisiana sometime in the early 1940's. So, when his mother named him "Ansell Edme" it was because it translated from the French to mean "Noble Prosperous Protector". But AE didn't care much for the translation horseshit nor the heritage nor his mother's choice of a name so he just went by "AE"

CL had called him from the plane on his way back from St Maarten. So AE left his home in Louisiana and drove to Houston to the main office to discuss the plans for the project. They discussed the plan and went over among other things: The basic pipeline route, the working direction, either West to East or East to West, how many spreads would be required, which ports the equipment would come to, where the pipe would be shipped, where the camps would be located along the route and a host of other minor details.

When they had finished CL asked AE "do you think you can convince three-finger to come? That is one hard working son of a bitch" CL said. " I don't know. He thinks you rather skinned him out of some of his completion bonus money last time" AE told him.

"Tell him he will get twice the bonus of anybody else" CL said thinking rather highly of his generosity "Yeah well I really don't think that's going to get it CL" AE said with a grin "Well then what would?" CL asked with a very slight crackle in his voice

AE could see CL was starting to get just a little desperate. AE was smart enough to know he could not do this project by himself and he needed three-finger just as much as CL did. But he wanted to see CL stew in his own juice for a bit because of how he had treated three-finger after a very successful project, and if by letting CL sweat a little, he could help his friend get a better deal, then all the better. "Maybe a sign on bonus? CL continued "What do you think?" I really don't know I'll have to ask him" Or maybe if you just pay him what he thinks you owe him" AE said "That would be a good start"

"Tell him he's got both. Both double bonus and the $250,000 he thinks I owe him" CL said as he was distracted by some commotion in the outer office. "Ok good now that's what I'm talking about!" AE exclaimed "See you later CL" "Yeah... later" CL slowly said. CL was clearly distracted but sat there momentarily before he got up to see what all the commotion was about. AE got up rather hurriedly because he wanted to tell three-finger about his better deal he had just got. AE left the room ahead of CL. AE was a bit put out by CL's greed on the last one and even though he liked him he always thought CL as a braggart. He once said that there was a probably a plaque at the very end of the Alyeska Pipeline that read "THIS PIPELINE WAS BUILT BY CL WILKERSON....with a little help from a few others" Bravado and confidence were not short changed when it came to CL Wilkerson.

It turned out CL's distraction was being caused by a man in Western attire but clearly of Middle Eastern origin in the reception area. He was waving his arms around and talking very loudly and he seemed to get louder with each sentence. Sherrie the pretty young receptionist had never experienced such a "in your face" commotion and was overwhelmed and greatly intimidated. Apparently, he was upset over the pipeline route which came very close to the ruins of an old mosque and a graveyard that included his ancestors He was demanding something be done about it. He looked as if he was on the verge of getting violent. Unfortunately for him he took the wrong tact to protest and basically just came to the wrong place to be acting that way.

AE was fully intending on just walking out of the building right past all the hollering. and let "Mr. Wilkerson" deal with his own problem. He was just about to walk by the man when he looked over at a very terrified Sherrie. I guess the sight of a terrified pretty young girl, hit AE in the wrong place.

AE never said a word he just grabbed the guy by both his belt and his collar from behind and ran him head first out the double glass doors. Cracking both the glass in the door and the man's head. The man crumpled to the floor unconscious in the hallway the fight was over in about 5 seconds. As AE stepped over the man on his way out of the building he looked toward Sherrie and said, "tell CL I'm sorry about his door" and he proceeded to walk toward the elevator. Sherrie slowly raised her hand and said in a very shaky voice "Thank you."

By this time CL was in the reception area and he said, "what the hell just happened out here Sherrie?" CL was asking a rhetorical question, because he knew very well what had happened in fact he had seen AE "escort" the man from the office. "Rather un-phased and nonchalantly he said, "call the building security" and as he turned to go back to his office. "Oh yeah and tell them they better call an ambulance too" he said over his shoulder. As he walked away he muttered to himself "I wonder where the hell this son of a bitch got the information on this pipeline route so quickly" I guess A-rabs telling A-rabs that's how" as he answered his own question.

15

CHAPTER FOUR

Cornelius and Jacob

As CL returned to his office the main phone rang and Sherrie answered, "CL Wilkerson may I help you?" her voice still a little shaky. "Sherrie how are you is everything all right? you sound upset." The voice said, "Things are fine Mrs. Wilkerson." On the line was none other than one Margret J Wilkerson or at least that was once her name 25 years ago. It was now Margret Peabody after her remarriage several years prior. CL's third wife and the only one that he had any children with, one son. CL often blamed her and rightfully so for the poor relationship he had with his son. She had moved back to Connecticut after their divorce and took the boy with her and did her damndest to keep them separated.

The fight started between CL and Margaret from the very beginning. After the baby was born around midnight and when he knew wife and child were doing OK, CL returned to his office to finish some business. He intended on being away from the office for at least a couple of days to spend time with his wife and newborn son. Being out of the office like that was important back then because it was a time before internet, email, and cell phones. Many times when you were out of the office you were just un-reachable.

But when he returned the next morning he found that Margret had already signed the birth certificate and had named the boy after her father instead of his. She named him Jacob instead of Cornelius even though she had agreed to name him Cornelius. She did somewhat honor the agreement and gave Jacob the middle name from his father's side. So, his name became Jacob Langhorne Wilkerson and It doesn't appear CL ever got over it.

Jacob was a sensitive child, a good student, polite, courteous friendly and deathly afraid of his mother when she would go on one of her rants. She and CL divorced when Jacob was a year old and "that crazy bitch" as CL often referred to her was also something of an over protective mother. When the boy was little CL even had to get his lawyer involved to get her to honor the possession order she had agreed to as part of the divorce settlement. It was a real struggle in those early years and she and CL could not have a civil conversation.

The boy got to come to Houston and visit during a few holidays and for a 30-day period in the summer. But as he grew up Margret seemed to always have some sort of vacation or a trip or an excursion she was sending him on in the summer and it always seemed to coincide with CL's visit schedule. So, it is safe to say father and son were not close as he grew up because they saw little of each other. This troubled CL since it reminded him of the tempestuous relationship he had with his father and he had vowed to not let that happen to him. But alas, history seemed to be repeating itself right before his very eyes.

I think CL kind of gave up the fight with Margaret over Jacob the year Margret scheduled the boy to go to Chile on a school field trip. As it turned out that same year CL Wilkerson Pipeline Construction Company was awarded a pipeline construction contract in Chile. The project was well under way when the 24-person middle school group arrived in Santiago. CL had spared no expense in planning a party for the entire group at the 5-star Santiago Marriott. He had even contacted the school principal to make sure the group could attend an offsite and unscheduled function. Well it is CL Wilkerson we are talking about so the unsolicited $5,000 dollar check he sent to the principal in advance of his request "helped" the principal see things CL's way. That's just the way CL operated.

The group was booked in the Hotel Plaza San Francisco which was also a 5-star hotel. So as the group arrived CL contacted the Chaperone and invited them over. The Chaperone had heard about the agreement from the school principal so at least from her perspective all things were a "go" and she indicated this to CL. While CL was still on the phone, the Chaperone asked Jacob if he would like to talk to his dad but Jacob said, "not right now" This hurt CL and since they had not spoken in a while, but CL didn't make an issue of it and he just let it pass.

As happens in many family matters a misunderstanding can really cause a lot of hurt feelings. And such was the case between Jacob and CL. CL was so excited that he was beside himself of the thought of seeing is son. He had put together a surprise party for Jacob and all his "friends" who really were not friends at all but just school acquaintances. Jacob on the other hand was at that awkward stage in his life where he was embarrassed by his parents and could not see how letting his Dad meet all 25 school mates could be anything than a major embarrassment and a big disaster.

So, Jacob asked the Chaperone to call his dad to tell him they weren't coming to the Marriott. Jacob had not mentioned the invitation to any of the others on the trip. So, the Chaperone did as he asked and called CL back. After hearing that Jacob decided not to come, it put CL on one of his few whiskey benders. He felt that

Margaret had finally succeeded in turning the boy against him. And one and a half fifths of Crown Royal later, he passed out.

During the nights activities at the San Francisco and as the party atmosphere was in full swing. Jacob quietly approached the Chaperone and asked her if she would take him in the morning so that he could see his dad. She agreed. They arose early and took a taxi to the Marriott only to find CL had checked out and returned to the spread. Jacob felt that he and angered his father by not coming over the night before which really was far from the truth. But sometimes misunderstandings between adolescents and their parents get way out of hand. This was the case between them and the boy avoided his father based on the fear that he had angered his father. They didn't see much of each other than occasionally for the next few years. It was not until Margret's request to CL, after Jacobs graduation from college would it look like they would ever spend much time together.

"CL, I have miss Margret on line one" Sherrie said. "Who?" CL said, "Miss Margret your wife sir" Sherrie replied "That's EX wife Sherrie and thank God that its heavy on the EX. Well I wonder what the hell she wants" Damn a phone call from the ex-wife a nutty son of a bitch in my office, hell all I need is an enema and a IRS audit and this could be one of the worst days of my life." CL quipped not knowing that Sherrie had already connected them and that Margret was on the speaker phone and heard every word.

"Hello CL", came a voice over the speaker. I'll see what I can do to help you with that IRS audit but sorry I won't be able to help you with your enema" Margaret said. "Hello Maggie" He knew she didn't like to be called that but he did it for spite "Has hell indeed frozen over because if it has I was truly unaware" CL said.

"Enough of your sour comments CL I need your help" said

Margaret "With what?" "You sure as hell haven't before" CL said "With Jacob" said Margaret "Oh?" CL said waiting for the other shoe to drop "I'm concerned, concerned with his ambition and his motivation. He has been out of school for two years now and he does not have a job and I find out two months ago he has stopped looking" she said.

"And you and Mr. Magoo... I mean Mr. Peabody are out of ideas?" "exactly" she said. "well Margret for starters, it might have something to do with that $250 thousand-dollar Ivy league degree in Animal Husbandry you let him get. I warned you against that, remember? I said engineering, business, almost anything else, but you decided to let him be free and let him choose his own way. Well dear it sounds like he has chosen unemployment!" he said.

"I want him to come to work for you CL" said Margaret. There was a long pause on CL's end of the line. He was so stunned he couldn't utter a word. This was the woman who did her best to keep them apart for 26 years yet now out of the clear blue she is willing to turn him over to him. "Am I on TV?" "Is this candid camera? "I mean of all the weird things that could have happened to me today Maggie I've got to confess I didn't expect this" CL said rather astonished "CL, you have been on the spreads too long and your starting to talk like them" she said in a rather condescending tone "what-the–hell ever" CL snapped.

"OK Maggie I'll come for him tomorrow. I for the life of me will never understand why you have changed your stance but I'm not looking this gift horse in the mouth" he said. "No, come today come now, this afternoon" she said "I told you I was concerned and I am. CL as much as I never liked being your wife I know what you are capable of. I've seen you deal with people and your son needs the kind of direction only a father can give and I know how much you love him" she said. CL rather stunned was rather taken by the fact that Margaret felt that way about him.

But that relationship had been like a running gun battle for way too long for him to let her off the mat right now. So, he said. "Ok let me get this straight I guess what you're saying is please make a man out of my son because I have assed things up and spent 250 thousand dollars of your money on a degree that is as worthless as tits on a hog, he has no ambition, is unemployed, and is not looking for a job. Not to mention he has surrounded himself with bleeding heart liberals and queers. Am I correct?" CL said.

"You are still a just as vulgar as you always were" Margret said as she hung up the phone. CL called her right back and said "Look Maggie I'm in the middle of a huge project and I'm just going to have to send the plane for him. It will be there in a little over 3 hours. Please put him on it" "OK I will and CL" there was a pause on her end then she said. "Thanks CL" As he hung up the phone he stared out the window and said to himself under his breath " Damnit Maggie I must be in the twilight zone"

The Construction

The company was in a fevered pitch with everyone scrambling to get things mobilized. Things were shipped from the port of Houston with a third going of it going to Beirut and the remainder going to Kuwait. The sea ports were buzzing with activity and all of it had to be transported inland to the four project kickoff sites. Everything was going smoothly, and as Nassar had promised there was no Government Interference during the clearing customs nor mobilizing men and equipment across borders to their respective starting points.

The project was 1000 miles long and it would take all the resources of four whole spreads of men and equipment to complete it on time. That meant over some 1200 expatriates had to be hired, given physicals and work permits, issued airline tickets, flown over to Saudi, clear customs, and immigration, be transported to the camp sites and finally issued accommodation assignments undergo orientation and issued safety gear. Not to mention hiring 400 locals to help run the camps.

The first order was to construct the camps and CL knew that all of those activities needed to go smoothly or otherwise you could find yourself with a bunch of drag-ups just due to camp conditions and as such once people started leaving due to poor coordination of the camp. It did nothing short of escalate into a mass exodus and could easily turn into what's known as "suitcase parade" Above all of the things that had to be right was the accommodations and they had to have the right food. CL knew good people and if he thought you were the right person for the job he could put enough money in front of you to convince you to come. But he was one camp boss short, and right now that was a big problem. He called a few candidates all of which turned him down for various different reasons. He thought about it for a while then decided to ask for ideas from some of his key managers so he called AE and asked him "who can we get to run the Damascus camp to make sure it goes to plan?" AE said without hesitation, "why Joe Mag of course" "Joe Mag? said CL in a very put off tone "Are you kidding me? Is he still alive? And if he is he has to be older and dirt"

I just talked to him last week CL" he's up for the assignment but he is waiting for you to call and ask him" "Oh geeze" "what's the matter did he run out of hits to do?" CL said in an aggravated tone. "CL you know that's all speculation." AE replied. "Oh, all right I'll call him.

Joseph Newton Maggaconi was known to all as " Joe Mag" Joe was a portly Italian of average height with a distinct South Chicago accent. He always had the stub of a cigar in his mouth that he chomped on and seemed to be proud of the fact that he didn't smoke and liked to tell people so when they offered him a light. He was old school Italian and his folks came to America from the old country. Joe was friendly and really a rather chatty type but after all that talk he did no one really knew Joe very well. Or of his personal business anyway. That's because he didn't tell you much about himself. CL once said. "Hell, I knew that son of a bitch for twenty years before I found out he had a brother and a sister." Joe reminded all of us of someone who just walked off the set of an old Mafia movie.

He dressed rather plainly, was portly, always chomping that cigar and had that strained voice just about like Marlon Brando did in the Godfather movie. He was a great organizer and a spectacular cook. He had been on CL's projects for 20 years or at least the ones he wanted to be on. And after the projects were completed and everyone returned home he always invited anyone he thought very much of to come visit him in Chicago.

One day in the mid 1980's CL did just that. CL had been in Chicago on business earlier that day but was up partying all night on Rush street when at about 6 a.m. he surprised Joe with a visit. As CL was walking up the side walk to Joe's house Joe was coming out of the house and down the same walk. Joe recognized CL and greeted him warmly. Joe said he was going to the social club and asked CL to join him. CL still a little woozy from last night's party but he agreed to go.

They walked in the club and the place erupted as CL later explained "Joe was like the mayor in this part of town and there was no shortage of well-wishers". CL was impressed that he was so well liked and had so many friends. As the place quieted down, Joe and CL sat at a table. Soon Individual people would come to over to talk to Joe. Joe would always do the introductions "egghead bobby this is a friend of mine CL Wilkerson" and this went on for an hour with no one ever staying at the table very long. Joe standing up for some and sitting down for others. Occasionally two people would come over together and it was not until much later that CL recalled that when two would come over Joe would stand up and back away from the table a couple of steps then, the other visitor would come over and talk to CL while the first would be talking to Joe. Only by this time Joe was 5 or 6 feet away from the table. CL always found that a bit strange together with the fact that of all the people he met that day he never got as much as one "real" name all he got were nicknames.

By 11:00 CL had sobered up enough and wanted to take a cab back to the hotel and try to get some much-needed rest. Joe was just jabbering on like he always did. and reminiscing about past projects. CL finally stood up and told Joe thanks for the visit but he needed to go back to the hotel and crash for a while.

Joe stood up never stopped talking and started moving slowly towards the door. Joe asked one of the younger men to "hail a cab for my fried here" He kept on talking while moving closer to the door and when they got close to it CL took his chance to get away by taking a couple of big steps and finally getting out side to the side walk. Hunting for his cab by looking down the street in each direction. By this time CL was certifiably hung over and could not wait to leave. But he turned around to face Joe and noticed that the whole damn club had emptied and had come with them outside. There were only about 20 men and no women inside the club in the first place but before CL paid much attention, they were all outside standing on the on the sidewalk and some leaning against the building front.

CL thought it strange and muttered under his breath "boy these sure are some friendly sons of bitches" The cab arrived CL shook Joes hand and climbed in the backseat. Joe was there to close the door of the cab and was still Jabbering on about something. CL rolled down the window to tell Joe goodbye once more and sees that the whole crowd is telling him goodbye and waving at him. And it kept on after the cab pulled away. CL turned and looked back out the rear glass and no shit they were all still watching him leave and still waving. "Now that is a strange bunch" CL said to himself.

Joe was one of those people who had a dry and rather warped sense of humor. But everyone always got a charge from what might come out of his mouth. One day on a camp job CL and company had hired and brought in a bunch of new hands. It was lunch time and they all found their way to the chow line. About half way through the line this one kid starts wiggling around and looked like he was doing a funky little dance. Joe was behind the counter supervising the food distribution when he notices this kid. Joe chomping that cigar stub said, "Hey you, greenie, yeah you the one doing the St Vitus dance, what in the hell is wrong with you?" The kid said I'm sorry sir is there a restroom nearby?" Joe said, "why do you need some rest?" He said, "no sir I need to take a dump" "joe said I'm sorry son we can't help you. People have been coming in here all morning taking dumps and so we are out of dumps. Then Joe spoke up so loudly that just about everyone in the canteen could hear him and said "Listen up all of you numb-nutted bastards, people have been coming in here all morning and taking dumps, and I've been told that we are fresh out of dumps. So, do us a favor either don't ask or just leave us a dump" Then he told the kid, "Down that hall on your left then he muttered…. dipshit." Thinking he was serious the reactions of the new kids who did not know how to take Joe were priceless it was really better than the jokes themselves.

Several years after visiting Joe in Chicago, CL was lying in bed half asleep half watching the news on tv when he recognized a building. He knew he had seen before. It didn't take long for him to think "Damn that's Joes Mag's social club" Only it wasn't Joes' Club. Hell, it wasn't even in Chicago. it was the Ravatite Club and headquarters of the Mobster John Gotti. He turned up the sound as the camera crews entered the building and after watching a few minutes he thought "not only does the building look the same but the crowd looks the same".

CL stopped taking Joe's calls and when Joe finally called Charlie

Nixon to find out what was the matter with CL. Charlie called him and CL said "You know Charlie I figure my odds getting wacked by a mobster are greatly diminished if I don't know any mobsters. Besides Charlie you know that my life's plan is to live until I'm 90 and then get shot by a jealous husband! Charlie laughed and said, "Good Plan CL."

Charlie said, " Well is there any problem if I hire him?" CL said, "Not at all Charlie, it's your spread and you run how and with whom you want" I just don't want anything to do with the mobbed-up son of a bitch. "Joe is expecting a call from you CL and we need him on this project." So, CL looked past his issues with Joe Mag called him and hired him as the Damascus Camp Boss. Neither brought up any past issues. Ironically it seemed that they were both glad to be on the same team again.

The next few months could be described as a great deal of very hard work. The pipeline crews, once they hit their stride, were operating like a well-oiled machine making a mile and a half of progress each day and occasionally two miles per day. Mr. Bob was able to get the longest lengths of pipe for the biggest part of the pipeline and this helped tremendously with the daily progress.

In fact, progress for the construction phase for most the pipeline was even better than expected. CL Wilkerson was overjoyed at hearing this. One really couldn't tell what the source of his joy was. Was it the fact that it looked like he would make more money? Or was it an ego trip about fact that he felt he was smart enough to put the right people in right place to get the work done that efficiently. I guess it didn't matter he was happy.

Everything was going to plan except that between Damascus and Beirut. To get in the game as early as possible that segment was being constructed West to East or from Beirut to Damascus. The rest of the pipeline starting in Kuwait was being built in the opposite direction or East to West. Progress on the last 5 miles on the Damascus section was stopped on numerous occasions due to archeological finds especially as they neared Damarcus the oldest continuously inhabited city on earth. Mostly all that was unearthed were pottery fragments from previous settlements and some were quite old But when something appeared in the backfill swarms of archeologists from two universities and one government ministry were everywhere and that lay section was shut down.

CL Wilkerson was not as insensitive as you might think concerning cultural artifacts. In fact, he had a genuine interest in the history of the finds as well as their disposition and preservation. But CL Wilkerson was a pipeline contractor and his drive for progress certainly outweighed any interest in culture, so when he felt like these archeological operations were infringing too much on his progress and "getting in his pocket" as he said it was he decided to call Nassar. "Nassar you need to get these Archeologist pricks off my Damascus spread and it needs to happen sooner rather than later they are holding up the show." So, it was that CL Wilkerson got his way and he had every Archeologist removed from the site the very next day. He had AE move some hoes from some the tie in crews up to the ditch crew to make up for lost time. It was working and the ditch crews were making superb progress. It was now just a matter of a short time that the segment between Damascus and Beirut would be complete and ready for pre-commissioning and by now it was the last section to be completed.

CHAPTER SIX

Discovery!

CL Wilkerson was a hands-on owner, even though his father viewed him as 102 carat screw-up. He did learn quite a few things while he was on the spreads working for his father. Well he learned as much as anyone could learn while still keeping up with his partying and womanizing. But he had eventually learned a great deal.

Being that type of hands on guy he insisted on visiting the work progress. He and AE visited various crews starting from the back-end in Beirut to the front-end near Damascus. It took them 2 days with all the stops and the bullshit sessions to reach the ditch crew who was cutting ditch behind the pipelay since the sand was so unstable. They were getting very close to completion of the segment. As they arrived they were impressed at the rate the ditch crew was working. All except one trackhoe that is. "breakdown?" CL asked AE "Probably" AE replied.

AE walked over to the Land Cruiser and radioed the camp for a mechanic. As he walked back toward CL a mechanic truck appeared over the hill. "Damn AE you must be living right to get one that fast" CL said but it just sped on past the stopped hoe and then drove on past them as well. "Let's go up there and see what the hell is going on " AE said.

They pulled up and saw a few locals standing around looking in the open ditch. Inside the ditch was what looked like a large square stone that was just barely visible at the bottom of the ditch. Just about that time three finger came driving up to the location from the opposite direction and following him was the company's armed security force. "Get these rat bastards out of here" Three finger barked. The security dispersed the locals immediately. "Big rock Charlie?" CL asked, "No CL" Charlie said "I don't know what the hell it is"

Charlie "three finger" Nixon was only one who really had enough sense to make sure everyone left the area except the hoe operator, who was a local, CL, AE, Charlie, and Charlie's expat ditch Foreman Dewayne L "hog balls" Smith. Who got his nickname because he and most all the other hands had to shower in a common shower area. I'll let you use your imagination on how he got that name.

"Well Charlie why are we waiting?" CL said rather curtly "we are waiting for this" Charlie said. About that time an expat backhoe operator by the name of Homer Short came driving up. Charlie told the local operator to dismount and take the pickup back to the camp. "But why? We waited for this?" CL asked, "Because you never fully trust a local CL and we don't know what we have here " I've had plenty of buddies in Nam that trusted their locals only to either be killed by them or because of them. CL said rather sheepishly "Ok fair enough Charlie " Homer got in the cab of the backhoe and began lightly peeling away the sand from the obstruction. As he did it appeared to be a stone box that measured about 4 feet wide by 6-foot-long by about 2 feet deep.

The presence of a man-made object spiked all of their interests. Hog balls was in the ditch with the box trying to sweep all of the debris away, Homer was in the cab of the hoe, CL and AE were mesmerized and were staring in the hole and at the box. And Charlie Nixon was looking all around trying to make sure no one else was around to watch all of this. Homer finally gently dislodged the box from its resting place As Hog balls looked more closely he said, "Charlie I don't think it's stone" Charlie started to climb down in the ditch, and then he thought better of it and climbed back out. He then told the guys to" lift it out of there". Charlie was never one to put himself in a position of disadvantage in case of an attack and in a ditch bottom was one of the worst places you could ever put yourself in. So, they lifted it out of the ditch and placed it near the welded pipe on the right of way. And yes, it was a box, and a rather plain looking box at that with no engravings or markings as to who the owner might be. Charlie told Homer "Homer crank that boom up and bring that welder tent over here" Homer did as instructed and I everyone seemed to be caught up in the moment. And later after they had time to think about it were glad that Charlie Nixon had kept his wits about him enough to not leave the box out in the open.

Unbelievably so they felt the box secure enough without opening it and left it unguarded in the welder tent overnight. The next morning better prepared they brought a flatbed truck to the Right of Way. Charlie insisted that no locals be present again not even the much-needed security guards so it was up to the managers and even CL to quickly rig it, load it on the truck and cover it with a tarp and get it back to the camp and do all of it as fast as possible.

There was AE, Charlie, Homer, Hog Balls, and CL all there to do the work and when you have that many bosses you really do have too many chiefs and not enough Indians, and it was a real fiasco. CL's rigging of the box slipped and they almost dropped it. So, they set it down on the ground out in the open and re-did the rigging. They finally got the box on the truck and as AE tried to spread the tarp like you would a bedspread the wind caught the tarp and it flew away. They retrieved it and tried again AE not letting go this time and it almost pulled him off the truck with Charlie catching him at the last second. They finally got it loaded it onto the truck covered it up and was headed back to the camp with AE at the wheel of the flatbed and CL riding shotgun. As Charlie, Hog balls, and Homer were getting back in Charlie's Land Cruiser Charlie said, "Well Boys I think we could have done without those millionaire helpers, I don't know which of them is a bigger pain in the ass to work with" referring to AE and CL. They got the box back to the Camp and placed it a shipping container and locked the door. They all met later in the canteen to discuss when they would open it, still unaware of what they had just found.

"We need to do it during the day when the least number of people are in the camp" Charlie said. "you will always have locals since they are running the camp operation for the most part so since we don't have any spare welder shacks, we will need to take one of the welding crews off line and bring it into the yard".

"And the welders?" CL asked, "give them a day's rest, a day off" Charlie said "These guys have been busting their asses so If you give them a day off they won't even come out of their cabins all day" The next morning the welder tent arrived back at the camp. The group removed the box from the container and placed in the tent. They proceeded to pry the lid off and looked in. Inside the first box was another box only this one was ornately carved. They opened the second box and what they found inside it was almost beyond their comprehension.

THE TREASURE OF DAMASCUS

In the box that they found there were over 4,000 gold coins, several golden crucifixes', two jewel encrusted golden crowns one large one smaller, a few small paintings with gold overlay, many golden bracelets and cuffs, chalices, belts and statues enough to fill the box that was 4 feet by 6 feet by 2 feet deep to the top.

Both crowns looked more like helmets than they did crowns but it was evident that they were crowns indeed. The part that would fit over the head was lined with rows of jewels and the number of rows of jewels made them look like pomegranates. There were 12 golden chalices some plain and some very ornate. Two were jewel encrusted but all of them were solid gold. On top of everything else they had absolutely no Idea where a treasure like this may have come from, much less how it found its way on their pipeline Right of Way.

CL ordered the things be returned to the box and placed back in the container and they did or at least minus the one thin engraved bangle bracelet AE was now wearing on his wrist. They all forgot about it and AE probably had too. They were half bewildered and half astonished but none of them were thinking the same things they were before the box was opened.

CL said, "I've got to go pick up my son Jacob at the airport, see what you guys can find on the internet." The group went back to their respective cabins and they all searched the internet. Charlie did a web search and here is what he found.

"THE LEGEND OF THE LOST TREASURE OF DAMASCUS"

In 634 A. D. and during the conquest of Syria, the Byzantine city of Damascus fell to the Muslims to a man named Abu Bakr. The city had surrendered peacefully and the Byzantines were allowed to leave the city provided they left all of their goods and possessions behind. The Muslims entered the city after Byzantines departed, the Muslims accused them of a double cross since all things of value were reported to have been removed. The Muslim army caught up with the Byzantines and defeated them in a battle six days later. All Byzantine survivors of the battle were executed. But legend has it that no valuables were ever recovered. The Legend grew when it was reported by a group of Nomads that saw an unidentified group of people burying something west of Damascus the day before the Byzantines left the city. A sand storm the next day made it impossible for the Nomads to locate it. Through the years many attempts have been made to recover a lost treasure. The last official expedition was conducted by a French University in 1972 but nothing was discovered save a few pottery fragments from an earlier settlement near Damascus.

The question remains: **IS IT STILL OUT THERE? ----WAS IT EVER THERE?** Nobody really knows for sure.

CHAPTER SEVEN

Others Find Out

Bashar was walking home and his house was situated where he needed to cross the right of way every day. As he approached the right of way he saw the men standing around a big sandy box. He stopped short of the right of way not because of the box but because the camp boss had let him go early so that he could help his mother with chores and he didn't want the bosses to see him leaving early.

He got out of sight and saw the men put the box in a tent. The men then drove off and then Bashar continued his journey home. It just so happened that his uncle was visiting that night. Dinner was a time for children were to be seen and not heard. But halfway through the meal Bashar innocently whispered to his mother and brought up the news that something had been pulled from the ground today. The men were talking loudly as usual but then stopped when they saw Bashar whisper in his mother ear. "Come Now what is this?" His father asked. His mother cleared her throat a bit then said, "Oh Bashar says they dug up something on the pipeline today" What was it?" his uncle asked, "A box" Bashar said. Bashar's father was just as bewildered as the rest of his family but the Uncle had heard the legend about the treasure before and thought that this box could very well be it. They finished dinner without speaking another word about it. But afterward the uncle pulled his brother aside and said, "it could be the long-lost treasure of Damascus"

"Yeah do you think so?" the father said in a cynical tone "Just exactly what is the long-lost treasure of Damascus and who might have put it there?" " Well I really don't know but I know someone who does." "Come with me to the Mosque Tomorrow there is Imam that" …they were interrupted by Bashar, "Good night Papa good night uncle Ahab" Bashar said "I'll be here at 6 tomorrow good night" Ahab said and with that he went out into the dark night with a little spring in his step.

Bashar was a local 15-year-old boy who felt fortunate enough to get a job at one of the pipeline camps as a laundry boy. He would take the clean laundry and place it on the bunks for all of the hands. So, everybody in the camp knew Bashar he was well liked and was just a good kid. He really didn't know that he was making more money than his father was. He just cheerfully brought the money home each week and gave it to his mother. He felt good about being able to help his family.

But as kind hearted as he was he was still a gullible 15-year-old boy, who really fell in with the welders. But being around a bunch of pipeline welders was not without peril they were going to have fun at your expense. The typical brunt of their jokes was usually a green welder's helper who was at least 18 years old. The welders weren't malicious or mean by any stretch you understand and the truth be told many of the tricks they pulled on green helpers had been pulled on them when they were first starting out on the pipeline. Being the brunt of those jokes was kind of a rite of passage and they felt everyone must go through it to be accepted.

For instance, they would ask Bashar if he wanted to learn how to weld." Of course, he said "yes" and then the trap was set. "Well Bashar, one of the most important things in welding is how to properly wear your welding hood" began J.B. "Shag" Hendrick the welder foreman. "Yes, sir it's one of the most important things. So, what you need to do is wear this"…" No, its ok son I have another one" as Bashar objected to taking Shag's hood from him. "you need to wear this at least two hours a day around noon and look up at the sun to get your eyes properly adjusted."

So, for two weeks every day at noon there was little Bashar faithfully wearing that welding hood. And he was doing so in 110-degree heat just looking up at the sun. They all got quite a chuckle to see Bashar foregoing his lunch and his break just standing out there in the middle of the yard looking up towards the sky in that heat. They would come by the window of the canteen knock on the glass and say, "Atta boy Bashar" So the welders from the Midwest thought that 110-degree heat was hot but it was normal to Bashar. And he had already had his lunch so they weren't getting over on him like they thought they were. Finally, one-day it was exceptionally hot outside even hot for Bashar. Cal one of the welders told Shag "its hotter than a two pecker Billy Goat out there Shag, let the boy come inside." Shag said, "yeah I guess you're right" Just then he said, "OH-OH" Charlie Nixon was on his way to the canteen when he sees Bashar wearing a welding hood and looking up at the sun. "Damn welders" Charlie said. It had been 40 years since he had fallen for that same trick. "Now that's enough of that" Charlie said as he pulled off the welding hood from Bashar's head and gently took him by the arm and walked into the canteen. Everyone was scrambling like rats to get out of there. "Boys" Charlie Announced "If this shit happens again I'll run the guilty son of a bitch so far off it will cost him 20 dollars to send me a post card."

Of course, Charlie's threat was hollow and harmless. He came from a family of welders and he knew their value for the success of the project. He also knew the value of good morale in their ranks which meant jokes. There was a sense of pride that all pipeliner's had that was different than the rest of the working world. It centered on constructing something most people couldn't do or keep up with. Something of quality, efficiency, and speed. Even though Charlie did not agree with their choice of a victim of this joke he was kindred to the welders and would bend over backwards for them when he would be less likely to do it for most anyone else.

He bent down to try to talk to Bashar face to face but just couldn't quite get there "Who put you up to this?" Now Bashar was by no means a tattle tale but Charlie's imposing figure and deep voice turned his legs to jelly and he just said, "Shag." "Shag?" Charlie bellowed "That silly son of a bitch, I might have known it was him." "Ok Bashar all is well, off you go."

The next day at the Mosque Bashar's father and uncle inquired about the Lost Treasure of Damascus from the Imam. He said "The last time anyone asked about that was 1972 when a alcohological group from a French university came to dig, they actually had more information on its history than I do. "I will locate the paper. Come back tomorrow and I will share it with you." They arrived the following day to talk with the Imam and get the information he had promised them the day before. Only the Imam was not alone this time. Sitting next to him was Balthazar Al-Wadi leader of a terror group that would eventually became known as ISIS. They were greeted by the Imam but the rest of the talking and questioning was done Balthazar. They told him what they had heard about something being dug up on the pipeline. When asked where they heard it. Ahab started to answer truthfully and say that they had heard it from his nephew, but Bashar's father cut him off and said, "From a camp worker on the pipeline" "show me where" Balthazar said rather harshly. "We really don't know where "alhadi" which was the Arabic word for "Leader" just somewhere on that pipeline they are building is all we know" "Then contact your "camp worker and find out" as Balthazar continued to speak condescendingly to them. "Meet me here at noon tomorrow" "I'm sorry that won't be possible our camp worker must be at work." "He takes no noon break?" Balthazar asked. "Yes, I suppose he does ok fine we will be here." Ahab said.

As they left the Mosque, the argument started "Ahab your greed is endangering my son. By coming here, You and your Damascus Treasure have involved us with some very dangerous people." Ahab knew he had messed up but did not respond to his brother as they walked home. Bashar's mother went wild when she heard about tomorrow's plan. She started yelling and crying and refused to let him go with them. "Well at least let him go with us now and show us where they dug up the box then we will make an excuse why he is not with us tomorrow" Ahab said. She still refused. Bashar finally spoke to her very gently as he did and when he asked for her permission to do something. He asked to go with them before the evening turned into night. She just could not refuse her son when he asked her in that way. So, they departed. They arrived at the right of way but it looked very different than it did when he had seen it last. The ditch was completely dug and the pipe had been welded, coated, lowered in, and tied-in. A dozer was backfilling the ditch. The welder tent was gone. "Well" his uncle asked rather impatiently "I don't know it all looks so different" Bashar said "Oh, that's great" his uncle said angrily "what are we going to tell Balthazar?" "you started all of this and you need to figure out what YOU are going to tell him" Bashar's father said, "I'm sorry papa"

Bashar said "It's all right son lets go home so your mother won't worry about you any longer."

The next day at noon they met with Balthazar and they told him what had happened but he didn't seem as upset as they thought he might be. They were both surprised and relieved. "Be gone you are of no use any longer" Balthazar barked at them. They left the mosque in a hurry and couldn't believe their good fortune. As it turned out Balthazar was given better information from another source, a camp worker who saw the flatbed arrive in the camp carrying what looked like a box. So, Balthazar no longer needed to know where the box came from because now he knew where it was.

CHAPTER EIGHT

Jacob Comes Over

CL Picked up Jacob at the airport. As they were driving back to the camp Jacob said to his father "How much longer before you finish this thing Dad?" CL was preoccupied with the fact that he and his son were conversing as adults and how proud he was of that. Jacob said again "Dad how much longer do you need to be here?" CL said "well son the pipeline will be tied in next week or so, then it needs to be tested and dried so I would say about a month or six weeks before I can turn it over to the Saudis. But then there is the de-mobilization of the camps and equipment so it will be about three months before we are all completely gone".

"I was afraid of that" Jacob said "why do you say that son?" "Because yesterday there was a rebel attack on the government forces and many people are taking to the streets in protest of the government. It looks like civil war is on the brink of happening in Syria. Have you not been aware of any of that type of activity?" Jacob asked, "Well to tell you the truth son with 1000 miles of pipeline to build I can't say I have really been interested in much else. Although now that you mention it my security chief wanted to talk to me on an important matter yesterday, but I was preoccupied with something else and I didn't get to him." When they arrived at the camp CL pulled them altogether in the canteen. He introduced Jacob to the group. Charlie said to Jacob "Well Jacob it's good to finally meet you I've heard about you since you were a baby, if fact I think your dad told me about the first time you shit your pants and he changed your diaper." Being fresh from the Ivy league Jacob immediately thought Charlie as a vulgar hillbilly.

"Did you find anything Charlie?" CL asked Charlie said nothing he just handed CL a printout of his internet search. "Damn" CL said after reading it. He passed the paper to Jacob. Jacob read it and said, "What's this all about?" CL said, "I think we have found this and it's in a sea container here in the camp." Jacob crumpled up the paper, then CL said, "No let the others here read it before we throw it away." They took turns reading it Homer Hog balls and AE and were all astonished. CL took the paper and lit it with his cigar lighter and held it by a corner as he waved it up and down for a little while it burned before dropping it to the floor and stomping it out.

Charlie said, "Reminds me of the time we hit a Gook command post with a flame thrower, Gooks were running out of their hole on fire but of course we didn't 'put them out because we didn't give a shit about putting them out. Jacob looked bewildered. He couldn't understand how the two things were even remotely related. And he was frankly a little put off at Charlie's story. But everyone else knew certain things always prompted a Vietnam story. Later that afternoon CL explained this to Jacob. But meanwhile Jacob said, "Are you going to do the right thing turn this over to the Syrian Government?" They all started laughing "This boy sure has a sense of humor CL" Charlie said. "Do you not think it best to return it to its rightful owner?" Jacob said as the laughter died down "That's a noble idea Jacob but just how do you figure the Syrian government is the rightful owner?" CL said. "It was found on their land" Jacob said "So what?" CL said.

"It was found on their land because it was being hid so that it was not stolen from the Byzantines by someone who had nothing to do with the Syrian government of today. If you look at it your way it should go to the Roman government. But the fact is that the Roman government no longer exists. Did you not read the same paper I did?" "And I say the rightful owners are the ones who found it" "Ok so if what you have found is actually this lost treasure that has no living rightful owner then who finds it keeps it right?" Everyone answered Jacob at the same time "Right" OK so now you have it just exactly how do you expect to get it out of here? You have to cross the Lebanese border and you have to declare its contents to get it on a plane or a ship. Not to mention clearing US customs and I think jewels in a box is going to be pretty easy to discover, don't you?" "Yes, it would" Charlie said" "CL, I've been thinking about this and I have an Idea." "Well let's hear it" CL said rather impatiently.

"Pigs" Charlie said "Oh right, right " CL said as he immediately caught Charlie's drift "Pigs?" Jacob said how do pigs come to play in all of this? What do you think because the Muslims won't touch pork they won't look inside a slaughtered pig?" "No dumbass" Charlie said. "Boy CL, you said this boy had lived a sheltered life but son of a bitch" CL explained "way back long ago when your great grandpa was building pipelines, a gage was needed to be run through the pipe to make sure there were no buckles or kinks in the line after it was constructed and buried. So, they started with a steel body and put rubber disks on each end to make it seal when compressed air pushed through the line. And later something had to be devised to clean out all of the debris that found its way inside the pipe during construction and those were made of foam."

"I still don't understand" Jacob said. "Look hear dumbass " Charlie interjected "You know Mr. Nixon I really would rather be called something besides dumbass by you" Jacob said angrily "Oh you would like to be called something else, would you? Well son I'll tell you what and I'll make you a deal you stop being a dumbass and I'll stop calling you one, how about that?" Charlie said sarcastically. Jacob was a bit put off that his Dad did not get Charlie to back off but CL never said a word to Charlie about it and he knew Jacob was a borderline panty waist and needed toughing up.

"As I started to say before I was so rudely interrupted by Mr. Ivy league here, Jacob have you ever been to a bank with one of those drive up tellers? You know the ones where they shoot the canister over to you in that clear pipe?" "yes, I have" Jacob said "well this is the same principle only we are going to make our pigs containers to transport jewels instead of dollars" "Oh Ok I see yes that's a great idea but why do they call them pig's?"

"No one really knows for certain. There are several different theories on how they got the name but the best answer I've heard is that back in your great grandpa's day and when they were first used on a pipeline they weren't called pigs they were called "Pipeline Inspection Gages" used to check for dents and buckles in the newly constructed pipeline. "And pipe liners being pipe liners are always looking to call something by a shorter name so they became known by an acronym using the first letter in each word or "PIG's CL said, "AE can you get ahold of Mr. Bob and have him send us 6 steel body batch pigs, a 20 ' joint if 16" pipe a 4' x 8' sheet of 3/16" plate a dozen strap hinges, and some asbestos blanket material? Have him get it local if he can and get it here as a priority one please" "Will do CL " said AE as he was heading for the door to get to his office. AE called Mr. Bob and everything was sourced locally or nearby. Late the next afternoon the materials arrived.

CHAPTER NINE

Ship it to the Coast

CL recruited Shag the welder Forman to build the canisters but he told him nothing more. By noon the next day the canisters were complete and were made so that would fit inside the steel pipe body of the pig. CL directed the loading of the canisters. The asbestos blankets were used to wrap things into sort of a pouch and to protect them from the welding Then the pouches were placed inside the canister. The ends of the canisters were seal welded with Charlie doing the welding. He was a terrible welder and CL said his welds resembled "Racoon shit on a pump handle" than they did a pipe weld. But it served the purpose. Just before the last one was welded shut they realized that the large crown would not fit in the canister. Now what?" Finish it up put everything else in it we will just have to figure out another way for this piece. The canisters were welded into the pig bodies and looked l like ordinary pigs. They would not be opened until they cleared customs back in the states and were transported back to the construction yard in Houston. Now they needed to mark the rear of the pig to distinguish the ones with the canisters and the ones without. Obviously, with inspection they could be distinguished from the front but CL wanted a rapid way of identification. Looking at them from the front it was obvious they had been altered but a rear mark was required to make quick handling of the right ones without having to turn them around after they exited the pipe. CL's plan for receiving the right ones involved and loading them on two different vehicles. The pigs were marked with a notch in one of the rear drive cups and a small "racoon shit" weld from Charlie on the body. The "canister" pigs were placed with all the others scheduled to go to the right of way the next morning. The pigs would be launched at a temporary break near Damascus and would be received in Beirut at the end of the on-shore pipeline. Once they were received they would be transported by truck to a US flag cargo vessel and loaded on it.

The pigging operation started early the next morning CL, Homer, Hog Balls, Charlie, and Jacob taking the place of AE who stayed behind in the camp to do his day job took the pigs to the right of way. There were about 20 pig runs to be completed that day and Charlie instructed the testing Forman to run these, meaning the canister pigs, last and by doing it that way it would give the group enough time to drive to Beirut. After they dropped off the pigs they headed for Beirut and the pig receiver at the port.

Balthazar sent four gunmen in a truck to the camp that same morning to take the treasure by force. They waited outside for all the hands to go to the right of way and then waited another hour or so just getting the sense of the security patrols and the number of guards. At 8:30 am the drove to the gate and stopped for the usual security check. When the Gard approached the truck, they shot and killed him. They sped into the camp. The camp guards opened fire on the terrorists and one of the terrorists was immediately shot and killed.

The other three jumped out of the truck and entered the closest building they could find. It happened to be the canteen. Joe Mag was in the kitchen supervising the clean up after breakfast when he heard the first gunshots. Joe had been a veteran of the projects in Nigeria that CL had a few years earlier and knew that if you ever heard gunshots in a camp then you needed to get your weapon and get ready to defend yourself. While the gun battle was raging outside between the terrorists and the guards, Joe walked back into the serving area and grabbed his bag from under the counter. In the bag was a Ruger 22 caliber 10-22 automatic pistol with a homemade silencer. He screwed the silencer to the end of the barrel inserted a full 10 shot clip of steel tipped hollow points then racked one in the chamber checked to see that he safety was off and then lowered the pistol to his side.

The height of the counter was just high enough to keep the gun from view by anyone who walked through the door. Just then the door burst open and the three remaining terrorists with AK-47's came through it. One of them blasted a few shots into the ceiling to get everyone's attention but they already had Joe Mag's full attention. What they must have seen in Joe was a grey haired potbellied harmless old man who was probably scared out of his wits. It appears that they did because when they shouted their broken English to him he put his left hand up to his ear as if he was hard of hearing. They came a bit closer which was good for Joe because his eyesight wasn't what it used to be. They spoke to him again With his left hand again and his index finger extended Joe made the sign for "one minute" then when he saw that both of the terrorists were looking at his finger he raised his gun still signaling "one minute" and fired off two shots hitting two of the terrorist's square in the middle of their foreheads.

With one shot each the harmless looking old man killed them instantly. The third terrorist had stayed back near the door and when the shooting started, ran out the door and straight for the truck. AE was run-walking to the canteen hearing all the commotion when the terrorist running for the truck hit him with a burst in the stomach. The terrorist got in the truck that was still running and sped off toward the gate. The guards opened fire on the truck striking and killing the last terrorist gunman before he could drive past them.

Just after arriving in Beirut Charlie's satellite phone rang. It seemed to always be bad news when someone thought it urgent enough to call him on it. And this time it was very bad news. It was the security chief that went by the nickname of "Gonzo". He told Charlie all of what had happened with the terrorists and with Joe Mag killing two of them. He also advised him that Damascus was descending into chaos and that civil war was going to start at any time... Charlie listened and then asked, "Is everyone all right?" The chief said I'm afraid not Mr. Nixon they shot AE and he was taken to a local hospital but as I said the city is going to hell in a handbasket fast I am trying to find out which hospital they took him too. "Ok I'm on my way" Charlie said. "CL, we have to find some transportation.

I've got to get back to the camp we were attacked and AE has been shot." "Good Lord" CL said Charlie let's wait just a minute I've got Jacob trying to find you a helicopter. I could tell by your face while you were on the phone that it was pretty bad news. About that time Jacob came back and said, "Done it will be here in 20 to 30 minutes" You told them they were going to Syria, didn't you? CL asked. "Well no I guess I didn't mention it to them. "well you should have because some choppers are not registered in Syria and can't be flying their airspace. Let's hope you got lucky.

The chopper arrived and CL asked the pilot if he was registered to fly in Syria and he said yes, he was but he needed more money to do it. "How much? " CL asked. The pilot said "$1000 US for me and $500 US for the copilot" CL said," Well here is $2000 you guys figure out how to split it" and with that Charlie left his satellite phone with CL and got his ride back to the camp. CL said, " Damn I hope AE is ok, now let's go check on that pigging process" They arrived at the pig receiver location and looked at the pigs that already been received. None of theirs had arrived yet. Just then another pig arrived in the receiver CL could see as it was being pulled out that it was one of theirs. " Boys we've got and 1 down and have 5 to go" he said to Homer and Hog balls "We need a truck and we need to see where that US flagged vessel is docked and also find out how much longer they have before they disembark." The truck was easy enough to find there was a company rental right on site. Jacob and Homer took the truck and went to look for the vessel. Balls and CL stayed behind with the crew to see when the next pig came in.

Before Jacob and Homer returned to the location, all 6 of the pigs they had loaded with the treasure, had arrived. They didn't want to separate them from the rest just yet which proved to be a good idea. They waited there by the pigs for the truck to arrive. CL saw some sort of flash in the distance like light reflecting off of metal. He walked a few steps toward it then turned around to rejoin the crew. Just then Jacob and Homer pulled up in a flatbed. CL directed them to back the truck in so that it would be easier to load. Jacob said the flagged vessel was at pier 33 just about a half mile from here." What else?" CL said, "We spoke with the crew of the vessel and they said they disembark at midnight tomorrow." "Great that gives us plenty of time"

CHAPTER TEN

Captured!

Then out of nowhere came Baltazar and ten gunmen. They had been lurking in the shadows for some time watching and waiting to make their move. They started yelling in Arabic and Baltazar who spoke English rounded them up at gun point and directed them to a nearby warehouse. Baltazar had figured out that the treasure probably had been transported in the pigs. The trouble was he just didn't know which ones it was in and there were about 20 pigs that had been received. The pigs were stacked neatly near the receiver. The gunman took the four guys and the three-man crew who had been receiving the pigs into the warehouse. Then they made them strip their clothes off and put on Orange jumpsuits.

Charlie's helicopter arrived at the camp and Gonzo came out to meet him. He had located the hospital where AE had been taken to. The helicopter had not shut down so Charlie got back in and the headed for Hamad Hospital. Upon arrival Charlie told the pilot If I'm not back in an hour go ahead and make your return. The pilot agreed. Charlie made his way into the hospital and asked about AE. He didn't notice Joe Mag sitting in the waiting room at first. Joe was sitting in a chair but had nodded off. Charlie sat in the seat next to him and said softly "Joe" and Joe slowly opened his eyes. "hello, Charlie, its sure been one hell of a day" "I guess so Joe" Charlie said "How is he?" Joe said, "No news, he is still in surgery" Just about then a doctor came out and looked around for the Americans, Joe said, "this maybe it" and approached the doctor. "Are you with the American?" "Yes" said Joe. "I'm sorry to tell you he has expired" the Doctor said in a very low voice "Oh No" Joe exclaimed " "Damn" said Charlie. "his wounds were too many we extracted four bullets from his abdomen and he was weakened by all the blood loss. I'm sorry" The doctor said as he turned to walk away. "Thank you doctor for trying" Charlie said. "Will you stay with him Joe and make sure arraignments are made?" "I will call his wife but right now I have to go" Said Charlie. Joe said, "come outside for a minute" They walked to the pickup Joe had driven to the hospital in. "Joe handed Charlie the 22 with the silencer. "I don't think the attacks are over just yet Charlie, and you never know what you are going to run into" "Thanks Joe" Charlie said.

Joe waited several hours before the formalities were concluded and the body was prepped. The body was placed in cheap casket that looked like cardboard. The orderly came up to Joe and said" Are you with the American?" Joe said "yes" "then this belongs to you" he handed Joe a clear plastic zip lock bag that had AE's personal belongings. In the bag was his billfold, Joe immediately checked it and it still had about $3000 dollars in it so Joe assumed nothing else had been pilfered. There was his wedding ring, a matching mechanical pen and pencil set, a set of keys, a can of snuff and a thin gold engraved bangle bracelet. "What the hell?" Joe said as he looked at the bracelet but he could not figure out why it would have been on AE's person. "AE surly wasn't tuning in to a fag" he said to himself as he tried the bracelet on for size. Then took it off and put it back in the bag.

Charlie was walking from the parking lot where he had met Joe when he heard the helicopter being cranked up. He thought had it been an hour already? Yes, I guess it had. He got near it but the pilot did not see him and started to lift off Charlie waved his arms then took out his pocket intense flashlight he always carried and flashed the crew. The copilot saw the flash and that it was Charlie so they set back down to pick him up. They had an uneventful ride back to Beirut. They set down at the airport. Charlie had no way of getting to the seaport so the copilot offered him a ride if Charlie would help secure the rotor.

CHAPTER ELEVEN

They Meet Charlie Nixon

Now Charles Simpson Nixon also known as "three finger" was a man's man and was 6 feet 7 inches tall and weighed 275 pounds. He was one of those men who carried that weight very well and was in great shape for a man his age. He had a good Baptist upbringing and never smoked or drank alcohol. Even though he was nearly 65 he was still the consummate badass when he took a mind to be. Otherwise he was a soft spoken gentle giant who hailed from North Louisiana but spoke with no accent and could pass from coming from the Midwest.

He didn't care much for the nickname that accident in 1976 had laid upon him. But he didn't get upset when someone would slip and say it to his face. The ones that did were usually the Green hands. Usually he viewed green hands as "short time pansy asses" and unless you proved yourself by innovation or just plain hard work worthy of working on a pipeline with him you were thought of as being just another worthless clown and basically a write off.

If you did work hard enough to be approved by his standards he became a mentor, a friend and a protector to you. He was a practical man and really did only have three fingers on his right hand. He always introduced himself in the same way and immediately broke down any tension that may be present caused by his imposing figure. "Hello, I'm Charlie Nixon, nice to meet you and before you ask No I'm not related to that crooked son of a bitch"

As you might guess he was referring to former president Richard Nixon. But rumor had it that they were actually distant relatives. Charlie had been an Army Ranger and a Special forces veteran and had volunteered to go to Vietnam after 1-1/2 years of community college. He had spent most of his time behind enemy lines, he killed people with his bare hands, and rose to the rank of Captain after 3 tours in country. He rarely spoke of Vietnam he said it was "nothing more than a pain in the ass and a bad memory" but after being around him for a while you would get little tidbits of his experiences. And the was especially true when something reminded him of a Vietnam experience. He once said of the 25 men he went to jump school and Ranger school with that only 2 of them survived the war and "didn't come home in a box" as he put it.

On an earlier project during blasting operations a hawk flew by just as the charges were set off and the blast took place. Even though there was no "big explosion" during these operations sometimes a bit of rock and debris would get past the blasting mats, let loose and shoot in the air about 15 or 20 feet and it was always best to keep your distance from the blasting operation. Which he did.

Well, as that hawk flew low over the area of blasting, I guess to try to see what all the activity was about, the charges let loose and a little piece of rock flew up and hit the bird and killed him. He was flying so fast that he lingered in flight for a moment and landed in some nearby trees. So, there he was stuck in a tree.

"Poor bastard" 3 finger said "It reminds me of the time that we ambushed a Gook command post one night. We crawled up close and threw grenades into it killing them all. Now I'm an advisor attached to an infantry unit with a bunch of sorry ass pot smoking dumbass draftees. And one silly son of a bitch lights a stick of dynamite and throws it in the bunker" Don't ask me where a dickhead like that got a stick of dynamite much less why he thought he had to use it. I said, "look here dumbass, they are all dead" He said "just making sure Captain"

We moved back in the jungle that night to get some rest. The next morning, we returned to look for maps or anything else of value that we might use. Just above the entrance to the bunker was an arm of one of the gooks stuck in the tree branches. "Mr. dynamite" I forget his name I think it was Jessie from New Jersey or something like that, anyway he was a transfer from another unit. Says "look Captain gook parts!" And "hey can someone give me a hand over here? and just a hand I don't need a whole arm!" He got plenty of laughs from the guys in the platoon. I think some guys needed that black humor just to cope with the reality. I really thought I was going have a problem with this one. But It didn't much matter because this New Jersey asshole only lasted 7 or 8 more days before he was killed. Three finger said, "I thought to myself this little Gook just died for his country and he is here fighting for what he believes in... the poor bastard" And I'm here because I wasn't smart enough to stay in school.

So, in reference to the bird as a "poor bastard" it must have reminded him of Vietnam. And that's how you got to know the stories of three finger Nixon. A story at a time as something triggered its recall of an experience he had. Three finger got his name because he only had 3 fingers on his right hand. Thankfully he was left handed. He never initiated a hand shake. But he would always respond to one. I guess he felt some folks might be creeped out shaking half a big hand.

His father and his uncle were both pipeline welders in the 50's and 60's and tried their hand at pipeline contracting in the 70's. Three finger discharged from the Army after the war had ended and returned home. He was persuaded by his father and uncle to come to work with them on the pipeline. He wanted to use at least some of his education and not just do something he could have done without going to college. But he agreed out of respect for his dad and uncle. His father put him in the stringing crew and in short, he always grabbed the end of the pipe to help guide it in place, grabbing the pipe by the end was something the experience hands told him not to do rather than properly guiding it from the side of the pipe. Today rope tethers are used so the stinging crew guide it in place without having hands on pipe. But such was not the case back then. Because grabbing it by the end exposed your hand to a pinch point. That fateful day the stringing boom operators foot slipped off the brake and the tractor lunged forward consequently with a single point pick the pipe swung forward as well crashing into another joint already on the ground and you can use your imagination on what happened to his fingers being on the end of that pipe.

Charlie and the helicopter copilot pulled up to where the crew should have been receiving the pigs but no one was there. Charlie got out of the car and thanked him for the ride. The copilot drove away. Charlie looked around and then saw someone around the corner of the warehouse building adjacent to him. As the man got a little closer he saw that he was decked out in the Jihad garb. The man was walking toward him but was looking to his left at the harbor and all of the vessel lights. Charlie saw the AK-47 slung over the man's shoulder. He slipped back into the shadow and watched. The gunman was obviously on patrol, and the crew was gone Charlie's suspicions were rising. The gunman walked past and Charlie emerged to look at the site again. Then he saw one of the pigs that he knew they had altered. It was unattended and one thing he knew about CL is that he would have never let this happen. Something was wrong with this whole scene. Just then he heard what he thought was a muffled shout from the nearby where house. He crept over and peered through a window. He couldn't see anything because a huge crate was in the way. He looked around and saw a ventilation window on the second story. He had to get back in the shadow because the sentry was approaching again. He waited for him to pass by so that there was l little distance between them and then climbed up a nearby ladder peered through the vent window and looked down. He saw CL, Hog Balls, Homer, Jacob and the three Pig crew members all dressed in jumpsuits. They were on their knees and a gunman with a kerchief over his face and the whole Jihad gear was walking back and forth shouting. He had an AK 47 slung over his shoulder. Charlie counted, one, two, three, four, five, six, seven gunman including Mr. Loudmouth that were in the ware house Then since he had seen the sentry policing the outside he scrambled to the other side and saw four sentries one for each side of the building. Charlie got down from the building and hid along with pigs a few yards away from the side of the building. But being 6-7 he really couldn't hide very well he had the silenced pistol and could use it to take the guard out but he wanted to save the ammo until he really needed it because there were only ten shots in the gun and there were eleven gunmen.

The sentry was making his rounds on his side of the building and as he got close to the pigs Charlie knowing eventually he would be seen jumped the sentry. Charlie was skilled in hand to hand combat and quickly gained the upper hand. He grabbed the sentry by the head and snapped it breaking the neck. He drug the sentry near the pig pile and robbed the man of his AK. He knew not to use it because the gunman inside would probably kill CL and the rest. So, Charlie continued his stealth until he had taken down and eliminated all four sentries. He started back toward a side door in the ware-house when suddenly it swung open and another gunman emerged calling aloud for the sentry. Since the door swung out Charlie was thankfully behind the door. As the man appeared Charlie simultaneously closed the door grabbed the man by the collar from behind put the 22 up to his head and fired at point blank range dropping him immediately. He drug the fifth body to nearby to the same place. He waited for a while to see if anyone else would come out side outside. There were five gunman and Mr. Loudmouth left in the building and he knew it would be a stretch even for him to climb back up to the vent window and take them all at once without endangering the crew. But he thought to himself that since Mr. Loudmouth was clearly the leader one thing was for certain he would have to take him out first if he decided to ambush all six. Besides that rat bastard would probably have the presence of mind to start shooting the crew. After about fifteen minutes of waiting at the side door It finally opened and two more jihadis emerged They each lit a cigarette but stood in the threshold with the door opened. They were smoking and talking and obviously had not noticed that the sentry was missing. Charlie knew he had to act fast because it would eventually dawn on them the sentry was missing and they would make ready with their weapons whereas right now their weapons were still shouldered. But the door was open so he decided to deal with what he felt was the lesser of two evils. He had to make sure that the door was closed when he fired even if it meant putting these two guys on alert with their weapons. So, he threw a rock against the wall about 50 feet from where these guys were standing and pretty close to the edge of the building. They took the bait. They pulled their weapons and left the threshold and started walking toward the end of the building but at the last second one of them picked up a piece of driftwood laying nearby and put it between the door and the Jamb to prop the door open to keep from getting locked out since the doors locked when closed. "Son of a bitch" Charlie said to himself. Now he would have to make sure that door was completely closed when he fired otherwise it would carry the sound inside the building like a megaphone. This meant his original plan of ambush as they walked by would have to change. It also meant he would have to leave the safety of his hiding place and expose himself for the 20 feet or so to get to the door closed. If he made too much noise it could be all over for him before he got both of them with his 22 caliber pistol when the jihadi's had fully automatic Ak-47's with 7.62-millimeter ammo. "Talk about taking a knife to a gun fight" he said to himself.

The men got close to where the rock hand landed as Charlie slipped out of his spot and headed toward the door looking at where he was going and intermittently glancing at the men. He certainly couldn't run like he used to and he felt it took him along time to get to the door. He pulled the driftwood out gently and let the door close. He took two steps toward the men and away from the door. The click must have been heard by one of them because right then he turned around. But he no more got squared up with Charlie when the bullet hit him in the forehead. Charlie fired another shot and killed the other man with a shot to the back of the head. He decided to leave these two lay where they were and attend to the crew as quickly as possible. So, he took 2 clips from the dead jihadis guns. Then shouldered his "new" AK he had previously taken and scaled the ladder to the vent window position.

As he peered in again he noticed that Baltazar or "Mr. Loudmouth" was now holding a sword. The crew was now blind folded and their hands were tied behind their backs they were on their knees. It was obvious the crew were being told to reveal the location if the treasure or they would be beheaded. The jihadis were a little more spread out that they had been before so Charlie mentally went through the sequence that he would take to eliminate these creeps. He did not need full auto mode so he switched it to semi. He played the sequence over in his head one more time and then he opened fire killing Mr. Loudmouth first with a single head shot from behind. Then he shot the others in the sequence he had just practiced in his mind. One, Two, Three, Four. It was over with that quickly. He had gotten head shots on all but one of them. He called down to CL "is everybody ok CL?" CL said under his breath and genuinely relieved "Charlie Nixon, thank God its Charlie" CL called out " I don't know Charlie I'm blind folded, Jacob are you Ok? Balls? Homer?" Travis, Darrell, Jeff? " They all answered that they were ok. Charlie climbed down entered the warehouse and cut them all loose using a curved dagger he saw in belt of the Jihadi's laying in a pool of blood on the floor. As he cut the last pig crew member loose he heard a slight groan behind him. He walked over pulled out Joe Mag's gun and delivered a final head shot to the wounded creep as everyone watched. "Take that you no good son of a bitch" he said as he fired. They all looked at Charlie rather intimidated and stunned at Charlies wrath. "Ok boys' times-a wasting" Charlie said as he helped CL to his feet "Let's Go" Charlie said. But Jacob kept staring at the last Jihadi to die as his father took him by the arm and started pulling him toward the door Jacob could not seem to take his eyes off of him. Then he said to Charlie "You killed them all." "How many were there Charlie?" Jacob asked. "Eleven" Charlie said. "Where are the others? " Jacob asked again "Outside" Charlie said and paused for a moment. "In a pile" as he finished his sentence.

"I mean I've only heard about something like this in the movies Charlie." "Oh yeah?' Charlie said, "I got eight onetime in Nam one by one." As they walked toward the door. Charlie was first to go outside but stopped and peered each direction to make sure the coast was clear.

CHAPTER TWELVE

◆

All Aboard

"Homer get that forklift" Balls bring the truck" Charlie was used to giving orders like that. Charlie knew all those bodies would not go unnoticed for long and they hadn't much time. They separated the pigs from the rest and loaded them on to the truck. They drove the half mile to pier 33 and found the US flagged vessel they were looking for. They pulled up and talked to the yard master. Since they had no paperwork he contacted the customs agent. The agent was polite and filled out their forms for them even though he could not understand what these things were, and why the boys kept calling them pigs, or why someone would pay a premium to ship it on a US vessel.

Ship to? The customs man asked CL gave him the information for a Houston address "OK" said the customs man "Now I just need a passport to complete this". Their hearts sank as they looked at each other "Charlie later recalled when that hand asked you guys for a passport you looked like you didn't know whether to shit or go blind" Of course none of them had their passports because they were all locked in the safe in the camp as was the standard company practice. CL asked the Customs man "can we handle this a different way?" he said as he half way pulled a wad of cash from his pocket that was right around $10,000 in hundred-dollar bills held in a roll with a rubber band. "No sir I need a passport and bribery is a very serious offence here in Beirut." "Who said anything about that?" CL said immediately "My money wad was pushing on my nuts and I just needed to adjust it that's all, and you thought...?" "My apologies sir" the customs agent said cutting CL's explanation short.

"Now what " Jacob said rather sarcastically "I really don't know" CL said. About that time the first mate showed up to see what was going on and to get an explanation of what the pigs were and to possibly speed things up. "Any problem?" He asked, "I need a passport from them to document the identity of the originator and these gentlemen it seems are fresh out of passports " "Well he is right we can't allow it aboard without the manifest" the first mate said

Just then CL noticed the arm patch on the first mates uniform that gave the company name "Seaway Services" "Is this the Seaway out of Houston?" CL asked "It is" Said the first mate "Could I use your ship to shore?" "I suppose but why?' "Well Jack Kelley the President of this outfit is a neighbor and a golf buddy of mine and I'm fixing to ask a favor of him." Man, I'm glad I noticed that arm patch" CL said patting himself on the back a little "Yeah " Charlie said me to because we both missed those big ass letters on the hull of the SHIP!

And they were big letters indeed twelve feet tall at least and written right on the on the hull of the vessel "SEAWAY SERVICES" The first mate and CL went to the bridge. The first mate said "Here is the phone but I'm sorry I do not have the presidents home phone number". "That's OK because I do" CL said as he dialed the number. The local time in Houston was around 10 30 pm. The phone rang and rang but finally someone picked it up. It was Jacks wife "Judy?" CL began " This is CL and I really need to talk to Jack its urgent"

"Urgent?" She snipped "what did you do lose a fourth for your stupid golf game?" "NO Judy I'm in Beirut and I really need to talk to him please." You could hear her waking him up "Jack?" "Jack Its CL and he says its urgent". Jack took the line and said, "hello CL" "Jack I'm in a bind here and I need your help". CL said. Jack sat up in bed sensing the urgency in his friend's voice "What can I do for you CL? "Jack I'm in Beirut on one of your vessels and I need to get cargo aboard only I don't have my passport it's at the camp locked in the safe". "Can't you go back and get it? I think we have a vessel stopping there later in the week". "No, I can't Jack and it's too damn much to explain to you right now. Are you going to help me or are you going to keep giving me lame ass suggestions or what?" "Of course, I'll help you CL what do you need" "I need for you to contact the Daisy Maye and tell Captain Meyer that someone holding a US passport needs to go on record as the shipper for some Cargo I'm sending back to Houston" OK" Jack said "I need this right away, right now Jack" CL said. "OK Is the Captain nearby? let me speak to him" "Who am I speaking to?" Jack asked, "This is Captain John Meyer sir" said the voice on the other end "Captain Meyer this is Jack Kelley" "Yes sir" the Capitan responded. "Can you or your designees sign the manifest for shipping for me? Of course, I will indemnify you or whomever from any responsibility should it contain contraband and I will have a memo sent to that event on Monday if that is all right?"

"Yes, sir that is fine I will take care of it for you sir" " Thank you Captain and I think your Christmas this year will be much better than normal" Jack said, "Yes thank you sir" They hung up the captain signed the manifest and the customs man was satisfied and departed. The Captain called down and instructed the crew to put the pigs in the ships hold. CL said, "Thank you Captain, say you wouldn't happen to have a couple of spare state rooms, would you?" "I have one "he said "how many beds" "Two" he answered "Can we accompany you on your voyage to Houston?" "Yes, but you will have to have your passports to clear immigration in Houston" " CL was not going to be separated from the treasure again so he said "Ok Jacob phone that helicopter service. Balls and Homer, you can fly back to the camp and send our passports back with the pilot"

Balls and Homer arrived at the camp They told the pilots to shut down because they could be a while and to meet them in the canteen. Balls and Homer found Gonzo and had him open the safe so they could retrieve CL's and Jacob's Passports. After the attack, Gonzo had beefed up the security and the whole place looked like a fortress even though the project was near completion and truck after truck was bringing equipment back to the camp.

Homer and Balls went back to their respective quarters to wash up and then met outside to walk to the canteen together and deliver the passports so the chopper could get on its way. As they were walking Balls suddenly stopped. Homer said, "what is it?" Balls said, "the crown the large crown we didn't take it and its still here". Homer said, "I suppose we should send it too eh?" "Yeah I would think so but in what? I mean we can't just put it in a trash bag Lets go to the canteen and see if Joe Mag has a box we could use. Joe Mag greeted them in typical Italian style saying things in Italian and kissing them each on the cheek. Homer produced Joes 22 automatic that Charlie had given them just before they left "Joe, a present for you from Mr. Nixon. Charlie wanted to make sure he got this back to you Joe" and he wanted us to tell you it was needed and greatly appreciated he said thank you."

Homer handed him the gun to Joe. Joe frowned and acted like it was a hot potato. He hurriedly walked to the counter and placed it back under the counter on the shelf. I guess he did not want anyone to know he had it.

"Joe" Homer said "do you have a box you could give us?" One about this big giving Joe approximate dimensions. "Yeah sure, this way" so they walked to the far end of the canteen and pulled one out of a closet and gave them a suitable box "Thank you Joe" "Yeah" Joe grumbled "You know we could use a roll of paper towels too" Joe came unwound "did you two miserable bastards just wake up or what? Do you just think of one thing at a time? You, useless pricks" They were taken aback by Joes reaction to a request for paper towels until Joe said, "this way dickheads" then they realized that the paper towels were stored on the opposite end of the canteen. Joe had problems with his feet and he waddled rather than walked. Some of the young hands said Joe walked like he had a giant stick up his ass. Joe gave them the towels and they thanked him. Joe just grunted. Joe was a kind-hearted man that would help someone in need without hesitation of course you would not have thought that about him as grouchy as he was.

They obtained the passports from Gonzo and placed them in a yellow folder They used the paper towels to wrap the crown and use the rest to stuff the box. Then they shrink-wrapped the living dog shit out of the entire thing and headed for the canteen. "That's a lot of shrink wrap" Homer said "Yes, it is but hopefully it will keep prying eyes out of the box " Balls said "I think these pilots are ok but you never know do you?"

Joe Mag had cooked the pilots some veal parmigiana which he always said was his specialty and said, "if it doesn't roll your eyes back in your head then it's on the house" No one ever paid for food in the camp anyway but it was just Joes way of bragging on his cooking. The pilots were just finishing when Homer and Balls returned they handed the box to the pilots and told them there were changes of clothes for CL and Jacob. The pilots cranked up and flew off. They arrived in Beirut and drove the co- pilot's land cruiser to the seaport where Charlie CL and Jacob were waiting.

They delivered the box and scribbled in very poor handwriting was a note from Balls "Sending you something you forgot in the camp clean clothes for you and Jacob." Well that was nice of him." Jacob said, "I'm looking forward to getting out of these."

We still have a few hours before we go is there anywhere close we can get a drink?" I could sure use one how about you Charlie? "sure" Charlie said" "Just the major hotels serve alcohol" the pilot said, "there is a Four seasons hotel just down the street" he said "Well hell let's go" CL said.

They entered the bar of the hotel with CL ordering a Crown Royal, Jacob ordering a Heineken the pilot and copilot each ordered a an after dinner liquor and then they got around to Charlie and he said. "An Arnold Palmer in a tall glass with lots of crushed ice." You don't want anything stronger after all you have been through today Charlie?" CL asked. "No." said Charlie" I don't drink alcohol and in fact I never have."

"Holy shit Charlie all that time in the army and you're telling me not as much as one beer?" "Nope." Charlie said, "I saw my grandpa die of its effects at 58 and I made a promise to my mother." "Well hell Charlie I've made many promises to my mother some I kept some I didn't", CL said with a smirk.

"Well I keep my promises CL." Charlie said. You could tell he was clearly put off by CL's attitude. AE was dead and no one seemed to care. All CL was worried about that damn treasure. AE's death took a heavy toll on Charlie. They had worked together for many years and they were good friends. The fact that his friend lost his life over the treasure with CL now whooping it up, not giving AE another thought caused Charlie to almost snap.

"Here is to the find of a lifetime." CL said. "And our best days are ahead." That toast was the last straw for Charlie because there was no mention of AE. Charlie knew that if the treasure had not been discovered, AE would still be alive today.

He got right in CL's face and said, "look here you greedy little prick." "I've had enough, I've had enough of you, of the treasure, of the killing, of the whole damn mess." Charlie then turned and walked out of the hotel. CL was so self-absorbed he hadn't a clue what set Charlie off. They finished their drinks and returned to pier 33. Charlie hailed a cab to take him to the airport where we waited for the pilots to return. As the cab passed the warehouse, Charlie saw that the bodies had been discovered and police and ambulances were swarming. A policeman directing traffic made the cab stop momentarily to allow another ambulance to enter the parking lot. He then waved the cab on by and the cab driver slowly passed the warehouse straining his neck to see what was happening. Charlie sat silently in the back looking straight ahead.

CL and Jacob had boarded the Daisy Mae later that night and spent 34 days together at sea. CL told Jacob stories about his Grandfather and ones he had heard about Jacobs great-grandfather. They played a lot of cards and talked a lot about many different things. Father and son finally became better acquainted.

A porter came to the stateroom door and asked for their passports. Jacob cut the folder loose and handed them to the steward who was going to make copies. Jacob was all ready for some fresh clean clothes and continued unraveling the shrink wrap until he could get the box open. When he opened he was both grateful that Balls and Homer remembered that they had left the crown behind but, a bit disappointed because there were no clean clothes in the box. They had to borrow some clothes from the ship's crew. It was the first time CL had worn used clothes, but he seemed grateful and that humbling experience probably did him some good. They were stopped at the entry point by customs after the crown was discovered in CL's sea bag. But CL had enough connections in Houston to get the crown past customs without a hitch.

They returned to CL's Houston home in the exclusive River Oaks neighborhood. Jacob felt the neighbors rather snotty and soon became very bored with the place. CL thought that maybe a dog might help Jacob with what seemed to be a loneliness issue. So, he brought home a purebred Great Dane puppy and gave it to Jacob. Jacob said, "Thank You Dad but this dog is not for me it's not my type." So, CL returned it. "Let's go to the shelter Dad" Jacob said the next day. As soon as Jacob saw her he knew it was the dog for him. A cocker spaniel terrier mix that he named Daisey after the ship they had been on where he finally got to know who his father really was. After 26 years CL was finally able to buy his little boy a dog. Even though his little boy wasn't little anymore it didn't seem to make a lot of difference to CL.

CHAPTER THIRTEEN

Gopher Wood

Charlie Nixon went back to the camp stayed behind and made sure the de-mobilization was complete. He made sure the equipment made it to port but when the locals stole the occasional vehicle he turned a blind eye and did not pursue its recovery. Things were certainly slowing down for Charlie during this final part of the project so he spent more time in his cabin and on the internet. He did more internet searches on the history of the treasure and one of them speculated that the Christian Byzantines placed the treasure in a "gopher wood" box. "Gopher wood?" "Where in the hell have I heard that before?" He said to himself.

Two days later while he was watching the load out, one of the hands started talking to Charlie about a great flood that had just occurred in Thailand where they had laid a pipeline a few years before. "It happened exactly as you said it would Charlie." "That whole plain is now flooded." Jim Bob "Racer" Murphy said. "it's a damn good thing they finally listened to you." Charlie had recommended to the client that concrete weight coating be installed on the pipe that crossed the plain close to the coast to keep the pipeline from floating in case of a flood. Since pipeline buoyancy is simply a function of the weight of the water displaced minus the weight of any product inside the pipe, floating pipelines are only concern if the product is natural gas. Oil pipelines contain the oil which has sufficient weight to keep it from floating. The client disagreed but Charlie persisted. After several weeks of talks Charlie agreed to lay the 5000-foot section of the pipeline with weight coating installed without any extra cost to the client. He never mentioned this to CL because he knew CL would have had a big problem doing "work for free". But Charlie knew it was the right thing to do and six years later he was proven right. As he was walking back to his cabin thinking of that flood, it clicked to him where he had heard the term "gopher wood" before. He had his Bible based upbringing to thank for it." The flood, that's it! Noah's ark! "he said to himself That's were I've heard the word gopher wood before. He did an internet search for "gopher wood" when he got back to the cabin.

Here is what he found:

The Hebrew word "*gopher*" is used only once in the Bible, in Genesis 6:14. God told Noah to "make yourself an ark of *gopher* wood.

Because no one knows for certain what "*gopher wood*" means in this context, the King James Version simply leaves the word untranslated. But most modern English versions of the Bible translate it as "cypress" This is probably incorrect and is really only a guess supported by very weak evidence. Cypress is far from the only guess made by translators. Other trees included pine, cedar, fir, ebony, wicker, juniper, or acacia. The problem with all the theories are: First "*Gopher*" is not necessarily a tree that exists today. Many trees and plants have become extinct. Little is known about the kinds of wood available to Noah in the pre-Flood world. No one today ever has seen any pre-flood wood; because it was destroyed in the flood. Second, the identification of "*gopher*" with "cypress" or any other known tree, is based on Noah's supposed location of building the ark, which is also unknown. So, in summary, if "*gopher*" refers to a type of tree, it lacks sufficient evidence to determine its identity. So, no one on the planet has ever really seen gopher wood as it described in the Bible.

"Son of a Bitch no kidding?" Charlie said to himself. He thought for a little while to understand the gravity of the situation. He finally concluded that first, the box was evidence that "gopher wood" had survived the flood even though it may not be around today. Second, it would positively identify the wood used to make Noah's ark. And third, if the wood was extinct it could provide a sample for cloning and possibly help resurrect an extinct species. "Wow" he said to himself in disbelief. It was entirely possible that the box that contained the treasure was more valuable than the treasure itself! Certainly, in purely scientific or religious circles there was no doubt it would be more valuable.

Charlie strode out into the yard and looked around for the box. It was nowhere to be seen. He finally asked "Racer" if he had seen a small wooden box lately. "Yes I loaded some test fittings in it and loaded it out a couple of days ago. It's in a shipping container and probably at the port by now." Well, Charlie thought, he would just have to wait until it got back to Houston to locate it. But he was satisfied that it hadn't been lost or worse yet scrapped and thrown away.

CHAPTER FOURTEEN

A Curse is Revealed

CL's contract for the construction of the pipeline was about $1.4 billion dollars. He made almost $300 million. Having made the biggest score of his life, he decided to step down not long after returning to Houston and he made a reluctant Jacob the new company president. When CL moved to Palm Springs after his retirement, Jacob went with him and ran the company from there.

CL had been right about the fact that the contractor building the loading facility would be the one who delayed the in-service date. Nassar requested that Charlie take it over. He did and accelerated the completion by about two months. Nassar was pleased and sent praises about Charlie to CL. By the time Charlie left the country almost four months after the pipeline was complete, the Syrian civil war was in full swing and it had become a very dangerous place to be. After that Charlie didn't speak to CL for quite some time. The pipeline was finished the company made a lot of money and CL sent checks to Charlie totaling about 10 million dollars but, the checks went uncashed.

When CL and Jacob returned to Houston with the treasure, CL

was taken to court and sued twice over the ownership rights. But nothing ever came of any of the lawsuits, since no one could prove ownership. CL eventually donated a large amount of it to the British Museum the Louvre and the Smithsonian. But he did send Charlie, Balls and Homer an artifact each to remind them of the adventure. He gave Balls and Charlie a large solid gold cuff that was about 3 inches wide. And he gave Homer a gold crucifix since Homer was always trying to evangelize him.

Charlie gave his cuff to AE's widow. When it arrived she curiously tried it on, but took it off after only about 10 minutes. The next afternoon, she was run over and killed in the parking lot of a Piggly Wiggly by a drunk driver running from the police. Balls and Homer were given three million dollars each, thanks to Jacob's insistence to CL. Each of them retired to their farms in Missouri and Tennessee respectively. Balls 11-year-old grandson tried on the cuff after seeing it on a shelf when his grandparents weren't home. Six weeks later he was diagnosed with an inoperable brain tumor.

Joe Mag suffered a heart attack on the flight to Paris. He died the next day. CL did not attend the funeral but sent lots of flowers and his condolences to Joe's widow. Jacob attended the funeral on CL's behalf and Joe's widow insisted that Jacob sit next to her during the service. CL caught the small amount of TV coverage that was given to it due to all the known mafia figures in attendance. It was because so many known figures attended the funeral of such an unknown one. As CL watched it on TV he said aloud to Daisey, Jacob's new dog, "See I told you that son of a bitch was mobbed up." CL was right because it was a true Mafia event. But I don't think Daisey cared one way or the other.

About a year after his return to the United States, Charlie decided to visit CL in Palm Springs. He arrived at the Mansion of CL Wilkerson about 9 am and rang the bell. He was expecting to be greeted by some young girl in a French maids outfit. But instead Jacob greeted him wearing a huge smile. Charlie was glad to see that Jacob was with his father full time. Jacob said, "Hello Mr. Nixon" and gave Charlie a great big long bear hug like they were the long-lost friends that they certainly were. The emotion seemed to overwhelm Charlie for a moment and suddenly small tear welled up in the corner of one of his eyes. Charlie said, "damn I haven't cried like that since I lost Sandy" he sniffled a bit. Jacob immediately stood more erect almost like a solder at attention anticipating another bloody, gory Vietnam story and said,

"Who was Sandy?" Charlie sniffled again and said with a little crackle in his voice and another sniffle "she was my girl, my only girl." "Your wife? Or girlfriend?" Jacob asked "No dumbass she was the best damn dog I ever had. She was just a terrier mix but she was smart as a whip and she loved me until the day she died."

Jacob chucked and closed the front door. As they started slowly walking toward CL's study Charlie said, "You know Sandy could talk?" as they continued walking "Talk? Oh, come on now Charlie" Jacob said in disbelief "Yes, she could, she could talk, I'm serious as a heart attack…..I not shittin you a bit on that. Charlie said with confidence.

I used to tell her to sit down and she would sit and then she would look up at me with those big brown eyes and that cute little terrier beard and then I would hold up this pink rubber ball and ask her" Sandy, what color is this ball?" She would chatter her teeth a bit then she would open her mouth a little bit as if to talk without making a sound almost like a yawn and then all at once she would say.... "She could say pink?" Jacob interjected. "No dumbass she would say "rerr-row" which sounded like yellow." And I used to say to myself, "Just my luck I have a talking dog and the son of a bitch has a speech impediment and is color blind!" " Jacob busted out laughing and said boy Charlie I sure walked into that one!"

About that time, they reached the study where CL looked like he was asleep in his chair "Dad?" Jacob called "Dad?" But CL did not stir. " Look what the cat drug in Dad" Jacob said again' "Look who's here Dad". He started to get concerned because his father was typically a light sleeper. "Dad?" He said a litter louder. Jacob shook him a little then called to him again Dad? He called again, then Jacob looked at Charlie with a look of horror on his face and he knew his father was dead. Charlie said, "Well we need to call an ambulance". Charlie phoned the police and asked for an ambulance. Jacob set on the sofa completely stunned and staring out into space. Charlie asked Jacob if CL had done anything unusual over the last few days. Jacob thought about it "Well he had plenty to drink at the Gala two nights ago." " Gala?" Charlie asked, "Yes it was in honor of Dad's donation of the Crown to the museum". "He and the curator got a bit drunk and took turns having their pictures taken wearing the crown." Nothing else?" Charlie asked, "Have you checked on the curator?" Charlie said. Jacob said, "No, why would I?" "Just a hunch." Charlie said, "Can you check on him Jacob?" Charlie asked. Jacob called Mrs. J Rogers who had set the whole affair up. She answered and Jacob asked her if everything was all right with Mr. Finks the museum curator. "Jacob why did you call and ask me this do you know something I don't?" She asked. "Well no, I just noticed he and Dad had a lot to drink that night and Dad passed away today they are about the same age so I wanted to check on him to make sure he was all right.". Well Jacob I just got a call from his assistant and he was found dead this morning. Apparently, he died in his sleep" "Wow I'm sorry to hear that." Jacob said. They continued some more small talk for a few minutes before hanging up. Then Jacob turned to Charlie and said, "Damn Charlie he's dead."

CL's funeral was two days later. It was then that Jacob and Charlie heard about AE's widow and Balls grandson. They knew about Joe Mag already. After the service and the few minutes at the grave site Jacob and Charlie returned to the mansion. Charlie, for the first time in his life had a glass of wine with Jacob as he had his usual beer. He and Charlie engaged in the usual post funeral small talk about the service, the flowers, and the huge turnout of dignitaries. They then sat in silence for a few minutes. Charlie finally broke it up by saying "Jacob, unless I miss my guess there is something really bad wrong with that damn treasure." "Why do you think that Charlie?" Jacob asked. Charlie said " Well hell just look at all the dead." "AE and his wife, Joe, Balls grandson, and now your dad and Mr. Finks."

CHAPTER FIFTEEN

Greece and Patmos

"What can we do about it Charlie?" "Well for starters let's look on the internet and find out more about the people who supposedly buried that phony ass treasure." They found that the closest modern religion to the early Byzantines was the Greek Orthodox religion, whose history, traditions, and theology were rooted in the culture of the Byzantine Empire. "Looks like we need to go to Greece to find some answers." Charlie said. "I'll call the pilots and have them get the plane ready." Jacob said. They flew to Athens Greece. They started at the Monastery Meteora at Thessaly. They were turned away for three days before anyone would see them but finally on the third day a priest greeted them. They were ushered into a small room and proceeded to explain why they were there and to ask if they knew anything about the treasure of Damascus.

The priest had certainly heard about the battle and the possibility of a treasure but couldn't provide any more details. Although he did have a suggestion on where they might find some better information and he directed them to the church on Mount Athos in Greek Macedonia. They left and went to the church at Mount Athos. After a long drive, they found that they were not well received at this church either. I guess it was because it got few visitors outside of the small village and virtually no strangers ever came around, much less two American strangers. The priest there was indeed more helpful. He had indicated that legend had stated that the Byzantine refugees went against their Christian faith and started using witchcraft and the dark arts.

The legend indicated that a curse might have been placed on the treasure but, since the treasure was never found there was no evidence to support it. He did not know what kind of curse but he was confident that the refugees assumed a Muslim double cross would happen and if they did invoke a curse it was aimed at the Muslims. The priest arose and then as if to say, "Your time is up." He had them escorted out of the Church shutting the door behind them. Finding themselves outside and at another dead end they turned around and knocked on the door again, and again until one of the brothers answered the knock. "Can you ask the father where we might go to find any other information please?" Jacob asked. The brother said nothing and closed the door. After a about a 30-minute wait Charlie was thinking they may just want to admit defeat and return to Athens. They had at least confirmed that a curse was possible even if they didn't know on what or why. Just then the brother reappeared and said one word and then closed the door again he said "Patmos"

Jacob and Charlie departed and drove to the next village to sort out what they just heard and to get something to eat. They found a small café in town and entered. They place looked vacant there were no guests. The owner of the café came out of the back room and seemed very happy to have a couple of customers. They ordered the "dish of the day" Charlie could not recognize what it was but it was surprisingly tasty. The owner came over to clear the plates and tried his very best broken English out on them. It took three attempts before Charlie and Jacob thought they understood what the owner was trying to ask them.

"He is asking what brings us here I think" Jacob said. "To see a priest" Charlie said as he put his hands together like he was praying. "Ah yes, yes" and he pointed to the church on top of the mountain where they had just come from. Jacob said "Patmos?" just throwing out what the priest had said to him hoping the owner would recognize it. Jacob shrugged his shoulders and raised his hands near his face as if to say, "where?" "Ahhh Patmos" the owner walked over to the wall near the cash register and pointed to the Island of Patmos in the Aegean Sea on and old and faded map of Greece. All at once it clicked with Charlie and he said, "Of course the island of Patmos that is where John the Apostle got all those visions and wrote the book of Revelation." "Yes, yes" the owner said. Jacob then pointed to the church and said" church?" The owner said "No, Monk". They paid their bill of about $9 dollars and then left a tip under a newspaper of the of about $50 dollars. They bid the owner goodbye and thanks, and walked out. Just then the owner came out waving the money they had left for him wanting to return it to them as if they accidently left it behind. Charlie motioned to the owner to come closer and took the money from him and then handed it back to him and said" Thank you" The owner smiled in disbelief and said with a slight chuckle "Americans." And so, they drove back to Athens searched the internet from the Hotel and were finally directed to the Monastery of Saint John the Theologian on the island of Patmos. They decided to leave the car behind this time and booked ferry tickets the next morning to take them to the island.

It was a very long walk up the side of a mountain to finally get to the monastery. They were quite exhausted when they arrived. They knocked on the door and a monk answered. They were ushered right in this time after a few formalities and questions concerning their business they were taken to an ornate and elaborate drawing room. They sat there alone for about 15 minutes. They were a bit surprised when they were told that they would be met by the high priest of the monastery. Jacob told Charlie how the place "gave him the creeps."

CHAPTER SIXTEEN

A Mystery Solved

Just then the high priest entered the room wearing all his priestly regalia. He greeted them and took a chair next to them and said, "I've been expecting you." "You have?" Charlie asked. "Yes, I have for I take it you are the ones who found a treasure near Damascus?" Charlie and Jacob were a bit shocked at the priest's comment. "I must explain." The father said. "Why else would two Americans come all the way to this monastery on Patmos?" It has been reported that excavations are happening West of Damascus and I was told your business from the high priest at Mount Athos." "Yes, we are the ones father and we have a problem. We seek your help and guidance" Charlie said.

The priest listened to all what had happened to Charlie and Jacobs friends and Jacobs father. He leaned back in his chair and said "Well the legend has it that the people of Damascus had turned away from true Christianity and were involved in hexes and curses and dark rituals. No one knew that for sure in modern times whether it was true or not...well at least not until today. If what you say is true then the refugees, before they smuggled the treasure out of Damascus, did in fact introduce a curse on some items. "Yes, but not every item seems to be cursed" Jacob said, "how so?" said Charlie "Homer that's how he is not dead and was given an artifact the same as you and Balls were.' "What was this balls person given?" the Priest asked? "A golden cuff same as me" Charlie said, "And this Homer person?" The priest asked again Jacob answered, "a large golden crucifix." "The priest said, "So there you have it." "Have what?" Charlie said, "The answer to the curse of the treasure of Damascus that's what." The priest said. "I'm having trouble understating this curse father so could you explain it a little better to me?" Jacob said.

"Of course, it's quite simple. You see the inhabitants of Damascus after departing from the faith began to experiment with curses and witchcraft." "When the Muslims first laid siege to the city the high priest would have begun cursing any item that could be worn." "He would not curse anything else. For if the items were ever raided or stolen it would just be a matter of time before some of the guilty would try things on for size and death would be soon to follow." "But they were individual curses intended to put doubt in the minds of those being cursed to question whether a curse existed and that things could be explained as coincidence." "You see wearing some of the items would cause different afflicting deaths, some would incite heart failure others would cause cancer still others might cause a violent death of some sort and so on."

"Any of the items, even those that are cursed are harmless if they are just owned or maybe displayed as an artifact on a shelf. It is not until one tries to wear the wearable items does the curse manifest itself and become dangerous" "But why" Jacob asked "Revenge, Revenge from the grave perhaps" "They figured the Muslim invaders would find the treasure eventually". "Well it's my best answer" The priest said. Then Charlie asked, "Could you reverse the curse?" "Well the answer to that is Yes and No" the priest said. "Yes, because given the original curse a few of us around here have been able to undo curses". "But No because the original curse for this treasure has been lost to history many years ago". Jacob then said to the priest You know I still have 10 or 12 items left of that treasure that probably could be worn. Most of the treasure my father donated to museums.

"Could I send you the remaining artifacts?" Jacob asked the priest "Yes of course that would be nice for at least some of the treasure be returned to the ancestors of the original owners." The priest said, "Good give me your address and I'll send them to you just as soon as I reach Houston."

"We will discuss the details later" The priest said, "But I just want to be rid of all of that treasure as soon as possible" Jacob said. The priest gave them the postal stop in the town and with that Charlie and Jacob bid the priest good bye. They returned to Athens and then to Houston satisfied that they had solved the mystery of the curse.

Charlie contacted AE's son and had him return the bangle and the cuff. Jacob contacted Balls and told him the story and got the cuff back from him. They contacted Homer and filled him in on what they had learned. They sent chalices to Balls and AE's son in exchange for the wearable items. Jacob had Charlie box up the crown that had killed his father because Jacob could not bring himself to even look at it. They sent it all to the monastery on Patmos. Then Charlie returned to Louisiana and dropped off the face of the earth for about a year.

CHAPTER SEVENTEEN

End Game

Charlie had been recently diagnosed with a terminal cancer. He knew he had but a short time left. So, he embarked on a quest to visit, one last time, anyone who ever meant anything to him during his lifetime. At the top of that list was CL Wilkerson but he was dead but his Jacob was a close second so he went to visit Jacob in Palm Springs. As he arrived he looked around at its beauty of that part of California and he thought to himself You know maybe I should have retired here instead of North Louisiana. Then after a little thought he quietly muttered softly to himself "Naaww I'll bet the crawfish out here ain't worth a damn"

Charlie arrived and made it to CL's mansion. He noticed a for sale sign in the yard as he rang the doorbell. Charlie fully expected to be greeted by that pretty woman in a French maids uniform. Instead Jacob opened the door and said "Charlie how in the hell are you?" Jacob said" "Well, come on in" "Thank you Jacob" "He then rang for the maid. She was still dressed as Charlie had earlier guessed it in that French maids uniform. "That apple didn't fall from the tree I see Jacob, like father like son!" Charlie said as he looked over his eyeglasses at Jacob. Jacob said, "Aw Charlie she is just a holdover from Dad and she will be here until the house sells". "Good job Einstein I wasn't taking about the maid per se I'm talking about the way she is dressed!"

Rosie asked what she could do for them Jacob said "I'll have a beer and bring my friend "An Arnold Palmer in a tall glass with lots of crushed ice". "You remembered" Charlie said.

Jacob said "Charlie, what brings you to town? Running from the Law again? Ditching another widow woman? Or just tired of eating those crawfish?" "No none of that" Charlie said " Just making my last rounds to say goodbye to people that have affected my life. You and your father were at the top of that list Jacob and I'm sorry I didn't get to patch things up between us before he died. My last words spoken to him were in anger over AE's death and I never intended to leave things that way with him. I was upset with him at the moment." "Well Charlie if it is any consolation he finally realized why you were upset with him and he bore no grudge." "But what do you mean Last rounds Charlie?" Jacob said in a sympathetic tone. "Will you stay for a while" Jacob asked" I'll have Rosie make up a room for you."" No, I'm sorry Jacob I can't stay long I've got a plane to catch later this evening and I'm on kind of a undetermined schedule here" "Well I don't understand that because you just got here" Jacob said . Jacob knew then that something was up but couldn't figure out what.

"I have a terminal cancer" Charlie just came right out and announced as he hung his head a little bit. Charlie had always been in control of very difficult and dangerous situations and this was one situation that he was not in control of. He seemed more embarrassed than anything. He had been an Army Ranger and had served in the Special Forces. He had faced death many, many times with some more certain than others. But this one he knew would get him someday and to lose any battle was embarrassing to him. "Terminal? Who says so Charlie maybe you should see my Dad's old doctor before you throw in the towel. We will get you the best care available" "Thanks Jacob that means a lot but Mayo Clinic says so I was up there last week" "Bloody Hell" Jacob slowly whispered in disbelief. "Quit talking to those damn Brits, Jacob!, they are rubbing off on you!" Charlie said and with that it eased the tension that had quickly covered the room like a dark cloud. They both laughed a little.

Rosie re-entered the room carrying a tray with a beer and an Arnold palmer. Jacob said let's have a toast. " Rosie passed the glasses to both. As they raised the glasses Jacob said" To Charlie Nixon and our past adventures, to a friendship of a lifetime, and to the man that downright saved my life." They clinked the glasses and drank. Jacob took a sip but Charlie guzzled his right down. And with that Charlie set down his glass and started walking toward the door with Jacob trying to keep up with him "Slow down dammit" Jacob said. And since he was not tall enough to put his arm around Charlie's shoulder he settled for Charlies waist and walked him to the door. Charlie walked out and turned to face Jacob for the last time.

"You know Jacob on this one we were kind of like Indiana Jones builds a pipeline and solves a curse, weren't we?" Charlie said. "No Charlie, it was more like Charlie Nixon builds a pipeline, saves his friends lives from certain death and recovers the lost Treasure of Damascus figures out that the treasure is cursed, kills a few terrorists and all without an archeologist." Jacob said, "Yeah, I guess so we just had Fanatic Muslims instead of Nazi's." Charlie said as he turned to walk away.

"That's right we did not need an archeologist to find that treasure.... Because we had "Three" as Jacob stopped himself in mid-sentence "We had Charlie Nixon on our side" Jacob said as Charlie was walking away. Charlie stopped and turned to face Jacob again and said, "Jacob you and your dad had Charlie three finger Nixon on your side and I've always been on your side." "I know Charlie yes you always have been for dad just as you have been for me." "Maybe you should write a book Jacob and I'll guarantee you that it will sell at least one copy, well maybe 2 if I decide buy one!" He got in his cab and rolled down the window. Jacob was so close to the cab it looked for a moment as if he would climb in with Charlie. They said goodbye again and then Jacob slowly backed away from the cab. As the cab pulled away Charlie held up the back of his left hand showing 3 fingers like the men did on the spread whenever someone would ask, "who told you to do this?" They would hold up three fingers. Charlie was looking at Jacob as it pulled away but when the cab made the first curve in the driveway, Charlie didn't look back.

62 days later Jacob received the sad news that Captain Charles Simpson Nixon had passed away. And with him the identity of the gopher wood box was lost. The box was still in the yard with rusting fittings inside awaiting the wrath of CL's Yard superintendent Jack" Dusty" Blankenship. CL for all his shortcomings was pretty well organized and was a reasonably neat person. He did not tolerate his yard looking like a "Damn train wreck" as he put it. So, every couple of years and the time varied between intervals, Jack would go on a rampage and start tossing things that appeared to have no value. Anything metal was sent to a scrap yard and the proceeds were used to throw a barbeque dinner at the yard. So there the box was waiting its turn to be placed again in obscurity and most likely in a landfill someday.

Jacob after hearing the news about Charlie packed a bag and took the company jet to Lafayette Louisiana for Charlie's funeral. It was certainly a military affair with lots of flags and a 21 one-gun salute, two three-star generals, one brigadier, and many others who had either served with him or had been trained by him were in attendance.

Jacob saw Homer and he came over and talked awhile. Homer saw Charlies widow and brought her over so that she could meet Jacob. "Pleased to meet you ma'am" Jacob said as he offered his hand. "Call me Nadine" she said. "I'm sorry I guess I didn't know Charlie was married" "He wasn't" "We were divorced a long time ago in fact he told me the other day that we were divorced three times longer than we were married" "We were still young when we divorced and neither of us ever remarried. I guess if it hadn't been for those damn pipelines that took him away so often we might have remarried." "We had our daughter 15 years after our divorce and I thought he would stay home with us. But another pipeline came up and he was gone again. I used to tell him that he loved those pipelines more than us and it caused a lot of friction between us. I finally realized it was the best way for him to provide for us. He could have never given us the things he did if he had worked a 9-5 here in town. After he came home from the war he needed adventure and pipelines provided him with that. He loved it, he loved the work and he loved the people he worked with."

Jacob immediately noticed that Nadine was a woman who had taken very good care of herself and was still quite attractive even though she was in her early sixties. Her eyes were a cross between a steel blue and a light grey and they were very piercing. It was easy to see what Charlie had seen in her." I'm sorry to hear about your father Jacob." She said, "CL and I were not the best of friends but I know how much he loved my Charlie." "Yes, he did" Jacob said. "So, have you met my Sherrie?" No ma'am I haven't. "You two have a lot in common being raised by Pipeliners" Oh no, there she goes and she is leaving." Nadine said as she ran toward the car that was leaving with Sherie in it as fast as she could in her high heels. She couldn't flag down the car 'as she called after her "Sherrie, Sherrie Nixon" Nadine was not able to catch her daughter's attention and stopped short of the driveway. Jacob and Homer walked over to her "Oh Well soon enough I suppose." Jacob did not understand what she meant by that comment but did not pursue it. Nadine said "Well Jacob it was very nice to finally meet you I've heard a lot about you from your dad over the last 20 years. Thank you again for coming. Charlie thought the world of you and he told me so just recently" she said. Charlie used to say, "There is no possible way that fine upstanding Jacob is related to the rat bastard CL Wilkerson!" They walked together toward the cars and finally she turned to him and said. "You need to meet my Sherrie she is as beautiful on the inside as she is on the outside." "All the best to you Jacob I really mean that thank you again for coming as she patted Jacob on the chest" "I was honored to come Mrs. Nixon." "Nadine" she said.

CHAPTER EIGHTEEN

Sherrie

Now Jacob had been around long enough to know that when someone was described to him as Sherie just was it usually meant she was homely. He remembered the time that a lady sponsor at a black-tie gala that he and his dad were attending described her daughter to Jacob in that same way. Jacob told CL about the potential fixup and CL said "Hell no Jacob she is full of shit that girl is ugly with a capital UGG!"

"You haven't seen her yet have you? Well I have and that girl is so ugly it looks like her face caught on fire and her momma put it out with a hatchet!"

Jacob sighed a little relief because ever since his dad had passed away he could not remember anything about his father in times long ago. He was concerned that those memories were maybe just gone forever. But it appears they had returned, Jacob cracked something between a smirk and a smile.

Jacob returned to Houston later that day and he decided he needed to start looking for a house. It looked as if his dad's house in Palm Springs was already getting offers. He got on line and looked at a website with real estate listings in Houston and finally, bored out of his skull, fell asleep in the chair. Tomorrow was a big day for him. Even though he had recently been named company president, he worked things out of Palm Springs and had never met any of the staff in the Houston office. He was usually 15 minutes early for every appointment, but today he decided he would be a little late. He gathered up his briefcase and a small box with pens, flash drives and other odds and ends. He arrived and parked in the garage in his father's former designated parking spot.

He got off the elevator on his floor and walked up to the double glass doors at the entrance of the office. Then he paused for a moment not knowing if he was ready to go through all of his father things. He took a deep breath and walked through the doors.

And there she was, the receptionist whom he had talked to just twice on the phone once was a short call and on the other it turned into a brief chat. He had not talked to her much because CL usually dialoged with her. And with all that had been going on in the business recently, not to mention his personal life, his thoughts were elsewhere. He strained to remember her name "Cheryl? Shirley? He was certainly not prepared for her striking beauty as it hit him like a freight train, he was truly speechless and instantly captivated. She said, "Good morning Mr. Wilkerson" with a bright smile that seemed to light up the room for him. But he could not reply and he just barely managed to produce a half-assed, creepy smile.

He had heard about "Love at first sight" but he didn't put much faith in the fact that it really existed. Or at least not until now. Just then the phone rang and she answered, "CL Wilkerson Construction may I help you?" It gave him an opportunity to stop staring at her and let him regain a small amount of his composure. As he approached the front reception area and set his things down on the chest high counter, she was still on the phone. He looked around and noticed that a plant was obscuring the view of her nameplate. He wanted to find out her name to save himself the embarrassment of asking her having forgotten it. He felt that he should have remembered it after talking to her twice. But for the life of him he could not.

The smart receptionists seemed to always have a nameplate that was very visible to save anyone who visited the embarrassment of not remembering their names. The name plate was usually situated in the center of the counter so that anyone who walked in would see it immediately. But a package had arrived that morning and the UPS man had moved the plate to one side to accommodate the package he was dropping off. So that morning the nameplate was partially hidden by the plant that was always on the far left of the counter. Thankfully she was still on the phone but about to conclude the call. Jacob felt a flash of anxiety still not knowing the name of this beauty. Just then as she was hanging up he panicked and quickly moved the plant so that he could see her name....And there it was.... SHERRIE NIXON. It immediately caused him to flashback to what Miss Nadine, Charlie's widow had said to him at the funeral when he and Sherrie were unable to meet. Something he did not understand at the time but it all made sense now Mrs. Nixon had said "Oh well soon enough I suppose" Jacob felt a little taken aback since no one mentioned that Charlie's daughter worked there. She concluded the call hung up looked at Jacob and flashed that bright smile at him and when she did he felt his knees almost buckle he cleared his throat and then just cracked a big smile back at her thinking he may have very well just found his bride. The END...

AN EXPERIENCED PIPELINER'S DEBUT OFFERING OF A FICTIONAL TALE DURING CONSTRUCTION IN THE MIDDLE EAST.

J. K. NEAL LIVES IN HOUSTON TEXAS WITH HIS WIFE AND 3 CHILDREN OF INTRIGUE WHILE BUILDING A PIPE LINE

CPSIA information can be obtained
at www.ICGtesting.com
Printed in the USA
BVOW06*2031150118
505281BV00018B/24/P